He had a hollow feeling in his stomach.

The urge to run hit him, but he stood immobilized as he listened to heels clicking on the floor in the main office area. On reflex, he catalogued the weapons within range: his gun at his hip, his backup firearm in the ankle holster, the knife in his pocket.

Then the door swung open and a pair of familiar eyes, fringed with thick lashes, scanned the break room before they zeroed in on him.

Oh, heck. She was definitely *his* Lilly Tanner.

Yet she was nothing like the girl he remembered.

"Good morning, gentlemen." Her voice was a sexy purr, enough to make a man sit up and pay attention.

SPY IN THE SADDLE

DANA MARTON

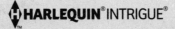

Recycling programs
for this product may
not exist in your area.

This book is dedicated
to my amazing Facebook fans and
my fabulous editor, Allison Lyons.

ISBN-13: 978-0-373-74780-1

SPY IN THE SADDLE

Printed in U.S.A.

ABOUT THE AUTHOR

Dana Marton is the author of more than a dozen fast-paced, action-adventure, romance-suspense novels and a winner of a Daphne du Maurier Award of Excellence. She loves writing books of international intrigue, filled with dangerous plots that try her tough-as-nails heroes and the special women they fall in love with. Her books have been published in seven languages in eleven countries around the world. When not writing or reading, she loves to browse antiques shops and enjoys working in her sizable flower garden, where she searches for "bad" bugs with the skills of a superspy and vanquishes them with the agility of a commando soldier. Every day in her garden is a thriller. To find more information on her books, please visit www.danamarton.com. She loves to hear from her readers and can be reached via email at danamarton@danamarton.com.

Books by Dana Marton

HARLEQUIN INTRIGUE

*Mission: Redemption
**Defending the Crown
***HQ: Texas

CAST OF CHARACTERS

Lilly Tanner—Shep Lewis was her teenage fantasy, even if he was her parole officer. Now she's with the FBI and must evaluate his team. She swears to keep her distance. But how can she, when he's sexier than ever?

Shep Lewis—When the girl who ruined his life shows up at his work, Shep couldn't hate the situation more. But Lilly proves herself at every turn, and soon he begins to appreciate the woman she's grown into.

Jamie Cassidy—An undercover operative with a dark past, Jamie and the rest of the team are watching the border to catch terrorists. He is related to Lilly and feels responsible for her.

The Coyote—A mysterious and powerful crime lord on the south side of the border. His true identity is unknown.

Brian Walsh—A creepy bar owner who has a hand in a number of businesses. Is he just a dishonest businessman or a true criminal who is trying to take over the illegal smuggling business on the U.S. side of the border?

SDDU—Special Designation Defense Unit. A top secret commando team established to fight terrorism and other international crime that affects the U.S. The group's existence is known only by a select few. Members are recruited from the best of the best. Shep Lewis is part of a six-man team from the SDDU who are stationed on the Texas-Mexican border.

Chapter One

As Shep Lewis, undercover commando, strode into his team's office trailer on the Texas-Mexico border with his morning coffee, his bad mood followed him. To do anything right, a person had to give his all—and he did, to each and every op. But it didn't seem to make a difference with his current mission.

He adjusted his Bluetooth as Keith Gunn, one of his teammates—currently on border patrol—talked on the other end. They all took turns monitoring a hundred-mile stretch along the Rio Grande, in pairs.

"Do you think they'll really send in the National Guard to seal the border?"

"They won't," Shep said between his teeth. "It would just delay the problem." For some reason, the powers that be didn't see that the National Guard was a terrible solution, which frustrated him to hell and back.

His six-man team had credible intelligence

that terrorists with their weapons of mass destruction would be smuggled across somewhere around here, on October first—five short days away. His team's primary mission was to prevent that. Switching out players for the last five minutes of the game was a terrible strategy.

They had the exact date of the planned border breach. If they could somehow discover the exact location, they could lie in wait and grab those damned terrorists as they crossed the river. The bastards would never know what hit them.

The National Guard coming in to seal the border could not be hidden, however. Which meant the terrorists would move their crossing to a different place at a different time and might slip through undetected. The sad fact was, even the National Guard didn't have the kind of manpower to keep every single mile of the entire U.S. border permanently sealed.

"The op has to be small enough to keep undercover to succeed," he said, even if Keith knew that as well as he did.

"Except, we don't have the exact location for their crossing."

"We will." But he silently swore. They were running out of time, and the stakes couldn't have been higher—national security and the lives of thousands.

There could be no more mistakes, no distractions. They had five days to stop the biggest terrorist attack on U.S. soil since 9/11. Failure wasn't an option.

Keith cleared his throat. "The FBI's guy will be here today."

"Don't remind me." Frustration punched through Shep. Everybody seemed to have a sudden urge to meddle. "Where are you?"

"Coming in. Ryder's cutting the shift short. He wanted to talk to the whole team at the office."

"More good news?"

"He didn't say. We'll be there in ten."

They ended the call as Shep strode through the empty office that held their desks and equipment, passed by the interrogation room to the left, then team leader Ryder McKay's office. Ryder had been on border patrol this morning with Keith.

Voices filtered out from the break room in the back, so Shep kept going that way.

"She burned down his house, stole his car and got him fired from his job." Jamie Cassidy's voice reached him through the partially closed door.

Okay, that sounded disturbingly familiar. Shep's fingers tightened on the foam cup in his hand as he paused midstep, on the verge of entering. His mood slipped another notch as old memories rushed him. He shook them off. *No distractions.*

"She broke his heart," Jamie added.

All right, that's enough. Shep shoved the door open, maybe harder than he'd intended.

He stepped into the room just as Ray Armstrong said in a mocking tone, "Must have been some love affair." He glanced over and grinned. "Hey, Shep."

Shep shot a cold glare at the three men, all hardened commando soldiers: Jamie, Ray and Moses Mann.

The latter two had the good sense to look embarrassed at being caught gossiping like a bunch of teenage girls. Jamie just grinned and reached back to the fridge behind him for an energy drink.

The fridge and wall-to-wall cabinets filled up the back of the break room, a microwave and coffee machine glinting in the corner. In front of the men, high-resolution satellite printouts covered the table.

This close to D-day, they didn't take real breaks anymore. They worked around the clock, would do whatever it took to succeed.

Yesterday's half-eaten pizza, which they were apparently resurrecting as breakfast, sat to the side. Jamie pushed it farther out of the way as he lifted the drink to his mouth with one hand while he finished marking something on one of the printouts with a highlighter.

"So—" He looked at Shep when he was finished, too cheerful by half. "Want to tell us about her?"

Shep stepped closer, in a way that might or might not be interpreted as threatening. They'd all been frustrated to the limit lately, and a good fight would let off a lot of pressure. "I liked you better when you were a morose bastard."

Ray leaned back in his chair. "He's mellowed a lot since hooking up with the deputy sheriff." He turned to Jamie. "She's definitely changing you, man."

And not to his advantage, Shep wanted to add, but that wasn't entirely true, so he didn't say it.

Jamie didn't seem concerned about the perceived mellowing. A soft look came over his face as he capped his highlighter. "Love changes everything."

"Really?" Shep narrowed his gaze at them. "Four of the roughest, toughest commandos in the country and we're going to sit around talking about love? What the hell? Are we still part of the top secret Special Designation Defense Unit, or is this now the Wrecked by Cupid Team? Have changes been made while I've been out?"

He believed in true love. He'd seen it work; his parents had had it. But he also knew that—like anything else important—it only worked if you gave it your all. People like him, and the other guys on his team, could never do that.

He wasn't the type to do things halfway, anyway. He either charged full steam ahead or wouldn't even start. Love just wasn't in the cards for him.

"Romance is the kind of—" he began, trying to be the voice of reason.

But Mo gave a warning cough.

He would. He was another recent, unfortunate casualty.

He looked Shep straight in the eye. "Love is nothing to be ashamed of."

Shep wished the best for him and Jamie, but in his heart of hearts, he had doubts about their long-term chances. Yet what right did he have to be discouraging? He laughed it off. "It's sad to see battle-hardened soldiers turn sappy." He shook his head, looking to Ray for support, a good laugh or some further needling in Jamie's direction.

But, in a stunning display of betrayal, Ray turned against him. "So what's this about your psycho girlfriend?" he asked between two bites of cold pizza, sitting a head taller than anyone else in the room.

If Mo was built like a tank, Ray was built like a marauding Viking—his true ancestry. Jamie, between them, was the lean and lithe street fighter.

They didn't intimidate Shep one bit. "We're not talking about me."

A roundhouse kick to Jamie, then vault on Ray, knock him—chair and everything—into Mo. That would put an end to all the smirking.

Except that Ryder, the team leader, had forbidden fighting in the office after an unfortunate incident when they'd first set up headquarters here. As it turned out, even though the reinforced trailer was bulletproof, the office furniture, in fact, was not indestructible.

So Shep threw Jamie only a glare instead of a punch that would have been way more satisfying. "She was a kid, all right? I wasn't her boyfriend. I was her parole officer. End of story."

"He never pressed charges," Jamie told Mo under his breath in a meaningful tone, obviously in the mood to make trouble this morning.

Shep threw his empty coffee cup at him. "Didn't anybody ever teach you to mind your own business?"

Jamie easily ducked the foam missile. "How about you tell us about her and then it'll all be out in the open? It'd be good to know what we're dealing with here."

When they built ski resorts in hell and handed out free lift passes.

"Any reason we're discussing Lilly Tanner this morning?" Saying her name only made him flinch a little. His eyes didn't even twitch anymore when he thought of her.

Ray suddenly busied himself with the printouts on the table. Jamie had a look of anticipatory glee on his face.

A cold feeling spread in Shep's stomach. "How did her name come up?"

He'd made the mistake of mentioning her to Jamie when they'd been on patrol together a while back. He hadn't expected that she would become the topic of break-room discussion. Jamie wouldn't have brought her up for gossip's sake. But then why?

"She's the consultant the FBI is sending in," Mo said with some sympathy. He might have been built like a tank, but he did have a good heart.

Shep stared, his mind going numb. Individually, all of Mo's words made sense. But having them together in a sentence defied comprehension. "Has to be a different Lilly Tanner."

The one he'd known over a decade ago had been a hellcat. He'd always figured she would end up a criminal mastermind or an out-of-control rock star—she had the brains and deviousness for the first, the voice and the looks for the second.

Jamie tapped the highlighter on the table and grinned. "She's the one. I checked when I heard the name."

He didn't like the new, cheerful Jamie. He was used to the pre-love morose Jamie who could curdle milk with just a look. As a good undercover commando should.

The only thing he liked less at the moment was the thought of Lilly Tanner reappearing in his life. The possibility caused a funny feeling in his chest. "They'll have to send someone else."

"Unlikely." Ray grimaced. "We've been read the riot act."

"Sorry about that." Jamie had the decency to look apologetic at least. "My bad."

He'd crossed the border and taken out someone he'd thought to be the Coyote, the crime boss who set up the transfer of terrorists into the U.S. Except the man Jamie had shot had been a plant. The Coyote had gotten away, and the Mexican government was having a fit over a U.S. commando entering their sovereign territory.

Hell, none of the team blamed Jamie. But now the FBI was sending in their own man...*woman*.

Shep closed his eyes for a pained second.

His team would either stop those terrorists

from entering the country with their chemical weapons or die trying. The last thing they needed was the FBI meddling and putting roadblocks in their way at the eleventh hour.

Ray shrugged. "D.C. city girl coming to the big bad borderlands. Give her a few days and she'll be running back to her office, crying."

Shep swallowed the groan pushing up his throat. The Lilly Tanner he'd known didn't run crying to anyone. He was about to tell them that, but gravel crunched outside as a car pulled up, then another.

"Ryder and Keith are coming in early," he told the others. Maybe Jamie was wrong. Their leader would have the correct information.

Keith, the youngest on the team, came through the door first, tired and rumpled after a long night on the border. He did the best with people they caught sneaking over. One of his grandfathers was Mexican. He had the look and spoke the language like a native. People told him things they wouldn't have told the rest of the team.

He looked around and apparently picked up on the tension in the air because he raised a black eyebrow. "What's wrong?"

Shep couldn't bring himself to answer. He sank into the nearest chair and reached for a slice of cardboard pizza, then stared at it for a second. He wasn't even hungry.

"The FBI agent who's coming… She's a woman," Mo said. "She's—"

Ryder pushed in. "I was just talking to the Colonel, too. Lilly Tanner. Isn't it great?"

Shep's jaw tightened. "How do *you* know about Lilly?" He shot a dark look at Jamie. Couldn't he keep his mouth shut?

But Jamie shrugged with wide-eyed innocence.

"She's Mitch Mendoza's sister," Ryder said.

A moment of confused silence passed as the men looked at each other, processing the unexpected information.

Jamie spoke first. "The one he's been looking for?" His sister was married to Mendoza, so this was family business for him. "I thought her name was Cindy."

"Got changed at one point along the way. You can ask her all about it when she gets here."

Mo clapped Jamie on the back. "Hey, that makes her your sister-in-law, doesn't it?"

A stunned smile spread on Jamie's face as he nodded. "Kind of. Yeah."

Ryder headed to the back for coffee. "Mitch found her just recently. Different name and everything, but it's definitely his sister. They had the DNA test done to confirm it."

Shep rubbed his temple where a headache pulsed to life suddenly.

Mitch Mendoza, another member of the SDDU, Special Designation Defense Unit, the large team that Shep's smaller group belonged to, came from a family destroyed by drugs. He'd been a teenager when his father had sold his little sister for coke. Mitch had been looking for her ever since.

And now he'd found her at last.

Except that through some bizarre turn of events, Mitch's Cindy Mendoza was Shep's Lilly Tanner. Shep swallowed. And she was coming here.

He tried to remember if he had any aspirin in his desk drawer. "They'll have to send someone else."

Jamie lifted an eyebrow, a warning look forming on his face. "She's my family," he said, in case somehow Shep didn't get that.

He did. *Shoot me now.*

"She can't be my Lilly Tanner. There must be a hundred Lilly Tanners out there." He stubbornly clung to denial.

"She's yours." Jamie extinguished that hope with ruthless efficiency. "I ran a background check on her when I got the name. Right age. Came from the juvie system. Right city."

Shep pushed to his feet.

"Where are you going?" Mo wanted to know.

"Taking a break." He needed an hour at the gym.

He needed a little time to clear his mind so he could focus fully on his work. His thoughts were all over the place, and he had plenty to get done today.

No distractions. He had to erase the picture that filled his mind: the seventeen-year-old bundle of holy terror that had made him quit the juvenile justice system. *Sort of.* Okay, fine, they fired him because of her.

But even as he moved toward the fridge to grab a bottle of water to go, another car pulled up outside. A throaty engine rumbled, sounding nothing like the team's SUVs. A car door slammed.

He had a hollow feeling in his stomach.

The urge to run hit him, but he stood immobilized as he listened to heels clicking on the floor in the main office area. On reflex, he cataloged the weapons within range: his gun at his hip, his backup firearm in the ankle holster, the knife in his pocket.

Then the door swung open and a pair of familiar devil-black eyes, fringed with thick lashes, scanned the break room before they zeroed in on him.

Oh, holy hell. She was definitely *his* Lilly Tanner.

Yet she was nothing like the girl he remembered.

Her full lips stretched into a smile that made Ray stare openmouthed. Shep considered throwing the water bottle at the idiot to snap him out of it. Then he realized that the rest of them were just as bad, staring at her, more than a little dazed. *Great.*

"Good morning, gentlemen." Her voice was a sexy purr, enough to make a man sit up and pay attention, nothing like the disdainful teenage tone Shep still heard sometimes in his nightmares.

She had stretched up and filled out, and somehow managed to look like a *Playboy* Playmate even in a straight-cut charcoal FBI suit. She wore her wild, dark curls pulled back into a no-nonsense bun, her five-inch heels a somber black, yet everything about her somehow spelled sex, which made Shep feel all wrong and uncomfortable.

She'd been his charge once. He was pretty sure he shouldn't be standing there thinking how she was the hottest thing he'd ever seen.

Good thing he knew too much about her to

fall for the new look. Hell, he even knew where her tattoos were—

He caught himself and tried to backpedal out of that thought. Too late. A strange heat flooded him.

She strode straight to him on endless legs, her hips swaying in a mesmerizing way. "Hey, Shep. Long time no see."

Enough roundness was happening in that skirt to make a man's palms itch. And her breasts, too, had come into their own since he'd last seen her. Definitely. His brain was short-circuiting, unable to reconcile his old image of her with the new.

"Are you going to introduce me to your friends?" she asked when she stood close enough for him to catch the light scent of her perfume, her head at a slight tilt, an amused look in her eyes.

He had a hard time recalling his friends.

"Ray Armstrong." Ray came around the table and took her hand, held it longer than necessary.

Keith deftly pushed Ray out of the way. "Keith Gunn."

She shook his hand, too, then Mo's and Ryder's as they came up to introduce themselves. Then she turned to Jamie. "You must be Jamie Cassidy, then."

Jamie stood with a bigger smile than Shep

ever remembered seeing on him, and walked
over to her, then enveloped her in a hug that
made Ray and Keith look decidedly unhappy.

"We're family," he said when he pulled back.
"I'm glad they found you. Now maybe Mitch
will learn to relax a little." He grinned. "What
are the chances?"

She stood a little stiffly, as if not entirely sure
of the hearty welcome. But she said, "From what
I've seen of him, very little."

Jamie grinned, then shot a *watch yourself*
look at Shep, who wished he knew where the
button was to project him into an alternate uni-
verse.

Ryder and Mo looked rather protective of
her, too. They both had tremendous respect for
Mitch Mendoza. Both would have laid down
their lives for him. Or his little sister, from the
looks of it. Ray and Keith, all googly-eyed, were
obviously in lust with her and didn't care who
knew it.

Shep swallowed in disgust. Less than five
minutes had passed since she'd walked through
the door. The disciplined, battle-hardened team
of six of the best commandos in the country
stood in shambles.

That was Lilly Tanner.

He drew a slow breath, careful not to inhale
too much of her perfume that wreaked havoc

with his senses. He was a well-trained under-cover operative. He could and would figure out how to stay away from her.

He stepped back, ready to leave the insanity behind, but her voice stopped him.

"While we're all together here, I do have some information to share." She paused, as if to make sure she had everyone's attention but of course she did and then some. "We have confirmed in-telligence that on October first, terrorists and their chemical weapons will be smuggled across this section of the border."

"We know that," Shep told her.

She went on. "This team is not large enough to monitor a hundred miles."

Ryder nodded. "But a larger force would be noticed. Then the transfer would just be de-layed or moved to another location." They'd been through this many times in the past weeks.

She held up a slim hand. "A small undercover team catching the terrorists would have been the best option," she agreed. "However, orders have been given for the National Guard to seal the area in question. They'll be arriving on the thirtieth. If you can't show results by then, we do need to be ready with plan B."

Ryder's face darkened. "It's been decided and approved?"

She nodded. "This morning."

"How long will they stay?"

"An indeterminate period."

"But an incomplete and temporary deployment?"

"Yes."

Shep watched her. "The terrorists will just wait them out. Or find another spot." Ryder had just said that, but it seemed she hadn't heard him.

She pulled her shoulders even straighter. "There's no guaranteed perfect solution."

Her not meddling in his team's business would have been perfect, Shep thought as Ryder asked, "And if we *can* pin down the exact transfer location within the next couple of days? In time to set up an ambush."

"Capture is preferable to deterrence. If you obtain an exact location, your team will be allowed to go ahead as planned with the apprehension on the first."

The phone rang out in the office area. Shep, already near the door, went to answer it, needing some space.

Jamie and Mo followed him. They were heading out to the border for their shift, so they went to their desks for their backup weapons and started loading up.

They had the date, but the tangos could change their minds. And catching even a regular smuggler could always turn into gold, if the guy could lead them to the Coyote.

As Shep picked up the phone, the others came out of the break room, too. He turned his back to them to focus on the call.

"Hey, I got those prints for you," Doug at the lab said on the other end. "They belong to one Jimmy Fishburn. Petty criminal." He rattled off the address.

Shep entered it into his cell phone GPS before turning back to the others.

Jamie and Mo were already gone. Ryder was heading into his office with Lilly. He glanced back from the doorway. "Anything important?"

"We got an ID on the fingerprints."

They'd been supposed to catch the Coyote when he came up to the U.S. for a medical procedure two days earlier. Instead, they'd chased and shot a stand-in. The driver had escaped, but they'd gotten his car and prints.

They'd never even laid eyes on the Coyote. The crime boss was pretty good at the game he played. Too bad. Because if they had him, he could give them the exact location for the terrorists' trip across the river. He'd know. He'd set up the transfer.

"You need someone to go with you?" Ryder asked.

Shep shook his head. He wanted to be alone

to regain his composure a little, and so he could swear loudly and at length on the way. "According to the lab, he's a small-time crook. I can handle it."

But Lilly flashed him a dazzling smile. "I can meet with Ryder later. I'll go with you. We can catch up on the way."

Just what he'd been hoping for. *Not really.*

If he'd learned one thing in the past couple of years, it was that you always played to your strengths. You figured out what your strengths were, built on them, made them even better and used them. You didn't go into your weak territory. Your weak territory was where bad things happened.

Women were his weak territory. Especially Lilly.

He opened his mouth to protest, then caught another look of warning from Jamie. She was his sister-in-law. Okay, that added another layer of trickiness to all this.

It wasn't as if he couldn't handle her. He could.

So he forced his lips into something he hoped might resemble a cool, unaffected smile. "Can't wait."

LILLY SAT IN the passenger seat of Shep's super-rigged SUV and tried to suck in her stomach while doing her best not to stare at him. Not that the arid Texas countryside provided much distraction. Low brush and yellow grass covered the land they drove over, a handful of farmhouses dotting the landscape here and there.

The cool, confident FBI agent thing back in the office had been a complete sham. Truth was, he made her nervous. Very. Not that he needed to know that.

"This Jimmy is our strongest lead?" She glanced at Shep from the corner of her eye.

Life was so incredibly unfair.

He hadn't changed any in the past decade. Okay, maybe a little. His shoulders seemed even wider, his gaze more somber. He had a new edge to him, as if he'd been to hell and back. But he could still make her heart skip a beat just by breathing.

No, she caught herself. There'd be none of that this time around. She was a grown-up, a self-possessed, independent woman. Or she would act like one, at the very least.

"Yes." He responded to her question. "If it pans out, Jimmy could be a direct lead to the Coyote."

She tugged on her suit top, wishing she knew how to hide the pounds she'd put on since their last meeting—*thank you, office work.* Being a cop had been bad like that, but working for the

FBI was worse. A week's worth of fieldwork could easily be followed by a month of debriefings, reports and other documentation, with her going cross-eyed in front of a computer.

His stomach was as flat as the blacktop they drove over, and probably as hard. Not that she'd looked. Much. She lifted her gaze to his face.

"Hot down here," she said, then winced at how inane she sounded.

She had tagged along to catch up, maybe even apologize for her past sins, but suddenly she couldn't remember a thing she'd meant to say. Shep still had a knack for overwhelming her.

He kept his attention on the road. "How long have you been with the FBI?" he asked in that rich, masculine voice of his that had been the center of her teenage obsession with the man.

"Five years. Police force before that."

He turned to her at last, his eyebrows sliding up his forehead. "You were a cop?"

"For a while. After I got my act together. My juvenile record was expunged."

He grunted, sounding a lot less impressed than she'd hoped he would be. As she tried to think of what to say next, he turned off the county road and down a winding lane, which led to a trailer park.

A hundred or so trailers of various sizes sat in disorderly rows, all in faded pastel colors. No people. Nobody would want to sit outside in this heat. Broken-down cars and rusty grills clogged the narrow spaces between trailers, garbage and tumbleweeds blowing in the breeze.

He drove to the back row, checked the address, then backed his SUV into the gravel driveway next to a derelict shed that sat between two homes.

"This one." He nodded toward a pale blue single-wide directly across from them that had its siding peeling in places. A tan recliner with the stuffing hanging out sat by the front steps.

When Shep got out, so did she. She caught movement at last—nothing sinister. Behind the shed, in a half-broken blue kiddie pool, a little boy was giving a graying old dog a bath. The dog didn't look impressed, but still stood obediently and let the kid dump water all over him.

The kid paid them no attention. He should be safe where he was. They weren't expecting trouble, but even if they found some, the little boy was out of sight and out of the way.

Shep looked at her. "What do you think?"

She scanned the blue trailer, mapped all the possible venues of approach in her head. "Anybody going up the steps could be easily picked off by someone in one of the windows." That would be the most vulnerable part of the exercise. "Do you need backup?"

"I can handle it." He checked his weapon with practiced movements, as if he'd done this a million times before. He probably had. "You keep an eye on the kid. Make sure he stays where he is."

She watched the trailer's windows. If anyone moved behind the closed blinds, she couldn't see them. "Any guess who the big boss is? Any clues to the real identity of the Coyote?"

Shep shrugged. "Our best leads have an unfortunate tendency to die before they can be questioned."

Which was one of the reasons why she had come.

While the six-man team was made up of the best commando soldiers the country had to offer, they'd been trained to fight, and fight they did. The body count was going up. She'd been sent to tone that down a little.

They weren't in the mountains of Afghanistan. Running an op inside the U.S. was a more delicate business. Border security was a touchy issue. International relations were at stake. They needed to catch the terrorists without starting a war.

Well, they weren't going to lose any leads on her watch. She glanced at the boy still busy splashing in the water, then something else drew her attention. A souped-up Mustang roared down the street.

The dog barked, then jumped out of the pool to chase the car. And the little boy chased after. "Jack! Come back!"

Something about the car set off Lilly's instincts, but there was no time to react, no time to stop what was happening.

Brakes squealing, the car slowed in front of Jimmy's trailer, and the next second the trailer's windows exploded in a hail of bullets.

"Get down!" Shep shouted over the gunfire and dived after the kid.

She'd never seen a superspy lunge like that, straight through the air, covering an unlikely distance in a split second as she took cover behind the SUV. She was on the wrong side to help, but at the right angle to get a look at the license plate, at least.

Shep went down, protecting the boy, rolling back into the cover of the shed with him as the dog ran off. The Mustang was pulling away already.

Her heart raced as she jumped up. "Shep!"

Was he hit?

Chapter Two

She couldn't see him. "Shep!"

Then he popped back into sight and shot at the Mustang, blew out a window as the car picked up speed, roaring away.

Lilly rushed forward and aimed at one of the back tires, barely seeing anything from the dust cloud the car was kicking up. She missed.

"You stay right here," she heard Shep call out, probably to the kid, then he was next to her.

"Call in the plate. Call the office." He rushed forward, up the shot-up trailer's steps. "Law enforcement," he called out when he reached the top. "Don't shoot. Are you okay in there, Jimmy?" He kicked in the already damaged door and disappeared inside.

She moved after him, glancing back as the dog returned and ran into the gap between the shed and the trailer next to it, back to the boy. One step forward and she could see the kid, his arms tight around the dog's neck as the animal licked his dirty face. Didn't look as if either of them had gotten hurt.

She pointed at him. "You stay there. Don't move. Okay?"

Neighbors peeped from their homes.

She scanned them and evaluated them for possible trouble even as she held up her badge. "FBI. Please go back inside."

She clipped the badge onto her jacket so she could dial, gun in one hand, the phone in the other, her blood racing.

The line was picked up and she summarized in a sentence what had happened, reported the license plate, listed the make and model of the car, and asked for assistance. Then she went up the stairs after Shep to help him.

She found him in the back of the trailer, standing in a small bedroom that smelled heavily like pot. Clothes and garbage were thrown everywhere. Their brand-new lead, a scrawny twentysomething she assumed to be Jimmy, lay in the middle of the floor. Frustration tightened her muscles as she took in the bullet holes riddling his body.

Shep crouched next to him, feeling for a pulse with one hand, still holding his gun with the other. He straightened suddenly, swearing under his breath, then speaking out loud what she pretty much knew already. "Dead."

He pushed by her, out of the trailer, and she ran behind him, noting the young mother who now had the little boy wrapped tightly in her arms.

"You," Shep called to a man in his late forties who'd also appeared, probably from a neighboring trailer, while they'd been inside. He wore denim overalls over bare skin and held a hunting rifle.

"This is FBI Agent Lilly Tanner," Shep told him as he hurried to his SUV. "She's deputizing you." He turned when he reached the car. "You sit in this chair—" he pointed to the recliner by the steps "—and don't let anyone go inside until the authorities get here. Do you understand?"

The man looked doubtful for a second, but then he nodded. "Yes, sir."

Shep jumped into his car, and she had to follow if she didn't want to be left behind.

She snapped on her seat belt, keeping the gun out. "What happened to standing still long enough to think and come up with a plan?"

"No time." He turned the key in the ignition.

"I'm not a sheriff. I can't deputize people," she said through her teeth as he gunned the engine. "You just left a crime scene to a civilian. Is this the kind of Wild West law enforcement your team is running here?"

"It's called doing what it takes." He stepped

even harder on the gas pedal and shot down the lane at twice the speed she would have recommended, people scampering out of his way.

A grim, focused expression sat on his face, his weapon ready on his lap, rules and regulations the farthest thing from his mind, obviously.

He was a different man from what she remembered. He belonged on the battlefield, not among civilians. She pushed the thought back. She'd barely been here; the determination was too early to make. She'd give him a fair shake. He deserved that much from her.

But she *would* have to make that determination at some point. Her mission here had an extra component his team wasn't aware of. She was to make recommendations whether to keep the SDDU's Texas headquarters in operation or have one of the domestic agencies take over their duties.

The law forbade U.S. military from being deployed inside the borders of the United States. The Special Designation Defense Unit didn't technically belong to the military—their top secret team reported straight to the Secretary of Homeland Defense—but they were a commando team, no matter how they sliced and diced it.

The few FBI and CIA bigwigs who did have knowledge of the SDDU were more than uncomfortable with them being here. And then there was, of course, the rivalry. The very existence of the SDDU seemed to imply that the bureau and the agency weren't enough to handle the job.

She was supposed to write up an evaluation and recommendation based on her experience here. But her judgment of the small Texas headquarters would have implications for the entire SDDU team. There was some pressure on her to come up with recommendations that would restrict their operations to outside the borders, like the military.

Pressure or not, however, she was determined to keep an open mind. Even if Shep wasn't making that easy for her.

He drove like a maniac. The Mustang was nowhere to be seen. It'd gotten too much of an advantage. Not knowing where it was headed, they would have little chance of catching up.

She cleared her throat. "We would have been better off staying and searching the trailer, I think."

Instead of responding, Shep made a hard left without hesitation when they hit the county road, and without yielding to oncoming traffic.

"How do you know they went this way?" she asked over the blaring horns and squealing tires, her right hand braced on the dashboard, her blood pressure inching up.

"Burned rubber on the road. Wasn't there when we came. They didn't slow to take the turn."

She glanced back but, of course, they'd long passed the spot. *Burned rubber*... She should have picked up on that. Would have, normally. She needed to snap to instead of allowing him to distract her.

He overtook a large semitrailer and nearly ran a car off the road in the process.

She had to brace herself again. "You can kill someone like this." She might have raised her voice a little. "What happened to waiting for backup? Also known as *standard procedure*."

Back in the day, he'd been a lot more balanced—the sane voice of authority and all that. Rules used to mean a lot to him. He'd had a ton of them. But not anymore, it seemed.

Which he further proved by saying, "We don't run things by the company manual here."

"No kidding."

God help her if the other five were like him. She pushed that depressing possibility aside and put on her business face. The bureau had sent her here to keep this wild-card team in line, and she was the woman to do it.

Shep might have been her parole officer at

one point. She might have had a crush on him so bad she hadn't been able to see straight, but a lot of things had changed since then. She was here to do a job.

She opened her mouth to tell him that, but he pointed straight ahead, cutting her off. "There."

The red Mustang was a speck in the distance ahead of them.

He floored the gas and did his best to catch up, scaring innocent motorists half to death in the process as he whipped around them like a race-car driver.

But when he finally reached the red Mustang, it picked up speed. So did he. Was he insane? Nobody could fully control a car at speeds like this.

She meant to read him the riot act, but he cut her off, once again, before she could have gotten the first word out.

"Take over the wheel."

"What? No—" But she had to grab the damn thing when he let go without even looking at her.

Then he took the safety off his gun, rolled down his window, pulled the upper half of his body outside and started shooting at the men in the car in front of them.

Of course, they shot back.

SHEP TRIED TO HIT the back tire, but the Mustang sat low to the ground and he was high up in the

SUV, nearly sitting in the window, so the angle wasn't much to work with. He couldn't shoot at the two idiots inside the car, which would have been easier. They needed them alive for interrogation.

"Coming in." He popped back onto his seat and grabbed the wheel from Lilly, who slid back into her own seat to make room for him, shooting him a murderous look, her full lips pressed into a severe line.

He floored the gas and rammed the car in front of them.

The Mustang nearly swerved into oncoming traffic.

Lilly braced herself on the dashboard. "Slow down! You're endangering civilians on the road. Shep!"

"Take over the shooting. It's easier for you to use your right hand." He needed both hands for the ramming.

"This isn't how it's done. Public safety always comes first."

When the hell did she turn all prim and proper? "The public is safe. Unless you're a bad shot."

She said something under her breath he didn't catch.

"Listen—" He rammed the Mustang again. "I don't know how you do things at the FBI, but this is not white-glove law enforcement. You're in the combat-boot section now. If you want to stay here, you're going to have to step up to the plate."

She unsnapped her seat belt, muttering something under her breath, then rolled her window down and leaned out.

He did his best to keep the car steady for her.

She shot at the tire, didn't have any more luck than he'd had, with the Mustang swerving. She leaned out a little farther.

The man in the passenger seat shot back at her.

She didn't even flinch.

Shep could see from the corner of his eye as she lifted her aim. And shot the bastard straight through the wrist.

"Good shot." He flashed her a grin as she pulled back into the cab. But then the smile froze on his face.

Crimson covered her ripped suit sleeve.

His blood ran cold as he watched hers drip. "You're hit."

He slammed on the breaks and did a U-turn, tires squealing, horns beeping around them as he plowed into the opposite lane, back the way they'd come. *Oh, hell.*

She was shooting him the megadeath glare. "What are you doing? Are you insane?"

If he was, he was entitled to it with her showing up in his life after all these years without warning. He straightened the car on the road. "Taking you to the hospital."

"The bullet didn't hit bone. It's not that serious." She held the bloody arm up, bent at the elbow, and looked under her sleeve for a few seconds before she flexed her elbow. She winced and tried her best to hide it, turning her head.

He stepped harder on the gas. *Oh, man.* He'd had her for only an hour and he'd broken her already.

Jamie was going to kill him. Mitch Mendoza, too. Mitch was probably going to torture him first. "Push your seat back. Head down, arm up. I'm going to get you help."

"I'm not bleeding out. Take it easy."

He couldn't. He'd been responsible for her in the past and that somehow stayed with him. Plus she was Mitch's baby sister now.

Dammit, he should have never let her come with him to Jimmy's place.

He glanced into his rearview mirror, but the Mustang had already disappeared. "From now on, you work out of the office."

"I don't think so."

Anger rolled over him. "If you didn't get shot, I would have those idiots by now." She had no idea how distracting she was.

"You could have killed us with your driving," she snapped back. "You could have killed innocent civilians."

He swallowed a growl, hoping to God they would sedate her at the hospital. He wondered who he'd have to talk to to get her knocked out for a week.

He drew a steadying breath and focused. "When we get to the E.R., you need to keep in mind that my team is doing undercover work here. We're consulting for CBP as far as everyone else is concerned."

"I'm not going to the E.R. Seriously." She paused for a moment before she continued, "If you want to, you can take me back to my hotel. I wouldn't mind changing clothes."

"You need a doctor."

"I have a first-aid kit in my room. It'll be faster. I go to the E.R. with a non-life-threatening injury, and we'll be there for the rest of the day."

He chewed that over. She was right. Not that he had to like it.

"Fine. I'll take you back to your hotel. But I'm looking at your arm. Then I'll decide if you have to go to the E.R."

She scowled and, even scowling, managed to look beautiful. "You were always bossy."

She was talking about the bad old days.

"I was supposed to tell you what to do. That was my job." And he'd failed spectacularly. He didn't like to think about that, so he asked, "Where are you staying?"

"Pebble Creek. Prickly Pear Garden Hotel. Right in the middle of town."

He knew the place.

He picked up his phone and called the office, updated Ryder on what had happened at the trailer park. With the license-plate info Lilly had already called in, half the team was already out looking for the Mustang, and so was local law enforcement, so that was good. They'd get them. Shep told Ryder the direction the car had been headed when last seen.

"How are you doing?" he asked Lilly when he hung up. They were reaching Pebble Creek at last and he had to slow a little as there were even more cars on the road here.

The small border town was getting ready for a rodeo. There were signs all over the place and billboards with images of cowboys and bucking bulls. The rodeo circuit was a big deal around these parts, a lot of outsiders coming in, which wasn't helping their investigation one bit.

"You're not responsible for my well-being," Lilly was saying. "I'm not seventeen anymore."

"Yeah, I noticed that," he said aloud, without meaning to.

A quick laugh escaped her, the sound sneaking inside his chest. Even her laugh was sexy, heaven help him. He turned down Main Street, drove straight to the hotel and pulled into the parking structure.

"Are you okay? Why don't you just sit here for a minute?"

She shot him a dark look. "I'm not going to pass out."

Good. Because he really didn't want to have to carry her up. He didn't think he could handle touching her.

They walked to the elevators together. He kept close watch on her from the corner of his eye. At least they were alone when they got on. Her bloody arm would have brought on some questions, for sure. But they reached her room on the third floor without running into anyone.

She had a suite, small but tidy. She walked straight to the closet and grabbed some clothes. "I'm going to clean up. Make yourself at home," she said before she disappeared behind the bathroom door.

He looked around more carefully. The space, like any hotel room, was dominated by a bed: king-size, plenty of room for two. He cut that thought right off and turned his back to the damn thing. He blew some air from his lungs. He shouldn't be here. He shoved his hands into his pockets and reassured himself with the thought that he was here only in a professional capacity, and this would be the last time.

He scanned the rest of the furniture: a desk and a table with chairs in the small kitchenette. Plenty enough for the week she would be staying.

The sound of running water drew his attention to the bathroom door. He bent his head, rubbed his thumb and index fingers over his eyebrows as he squeezed his eyes shut for a second. He so didn't want to think about the new, grown-up Lilly naked under the hot spray of water.

He did anyway. Maybe he had more self-discipline than the average Joe, but he was still a man.

She kept the shower brief. Long before he could have reined in his rampant imagination, she emerged from the bathroom, wearing soft white slacks and a pale green tank top that emphasized the green of her eyes. A nasty red wound, at least four inches long, marred her lower right arm. It still seeped blood.

She went to the closet again and bent to the bottom. She grabbed a jumbo first-aid kit, then came over to sit on the edge of the bed. "I wouldn't mind if you helped me bandage this up. I'm not good with my left hand."

The bed? With five chairs in the suite, she had to sit *there?*

He almost suggested the kitchen table, but he didn't want her to guess that she affected him in any way.

He stepped up to her, trying not to notice her fresh, soapy scent. "You travel with an emergency kit?"

She'd been a pretty haphazard person back when he'd known her, definitely not the Girl Scout type. More of a "let the chips fall where they may" sort of girl.

She popped the lid open. "I like to be prepared."

Of course, she was an FBI agent now. She'd probably been shot at before, even if he didn't want to think about it. Obviously, she'd lived and learned.

He looked at the brown bottle of peroxide in the middle of the box. "Let's start with the disinfecting."

The bullet ripped along her skin but didn't go through, didn't damage muscle, or not too badly. That was good. She was right—she didn't need the E.R. Although, it might have been better if a nurse was doing this.

He hadn't planned on seeing her in so little clothes that he would have to notice her toned arms. He hadn't planned on getting close enough to her to touch her.

But fine—he was a soldier. He could suck it up for ten minutes. As long as he didn't look at the curve of her breasts, which the tank top very unhelpfully accentuated.

"This won't hurt a bit," he said.

She raised an eyebrow. "That's what they always say."

He slipped into latex gloves and disinfected the wound then dabbed it dry. To her credit, she didn't make a sound. He leaned closer to get a better look at the damage now that dry blood didn't obstruct his view.

She held still. "So?"

"The missing swath of skin is too wide for butterfly bandages, but the gash isn't deep enough to really need stitches."

To her credit, she didn't say *I told you so*.

He put on antiseptic cream then a sterile pad, wrapped her arm in gauze. "It's going to leave a nasty scar."

"Good thing I'm not a photo model."

As she shrugged, his gaze strayed to her naked shoulder, to her soft, tanned skin. Feeling lust at this moment had to be wrong for at least half a dozen reasons. Trouble was, she had him so bamboozled, he couldn't remember any of them.

He cleared his throat. "Good to go."

She flashed a smile. "Thanks."

"Don't mention it." He stepped back.

"And thank you for…before," she added with a tilt of her head, her eyes growing serious. She filled her lungs, a consternated look coming over her face for a second. "I'm sorry if I was a difficult teenager."

Difficult didn't begin to describe her. "You were something."

She smiled again.

He didn't smile back. "And by that, I mean trouble. And it was pretty obvious you'd be even bigger trouble in a couple of years. I was just hoping we wouldn't be running in the same circles by then."

She watched him. "And here I am."

"And here you are." He drew a slow breath, and the flowery scent of her soap hit him all over again.

LILLY WATCHED THE wary expression on his face.

Being alone in a hotel room with Shepard Lewis had been her teenage dream. To have him here now seemed beyond strange, even if under vastly different circumstances than she'd spent hours daydreaming about back in the day.

She'd written *songs* about him, for heaven's sake.

She pushed all that away.

"You kept insurance on the car I borrowed," she said. Okay, stole. But seeing how they were practically colleagues now, there was no sense splitting hairs.

He shifted where he stood. "Figured you couldn't afford it. Driving without insurance is illegal. Didn't want you to get into more trouble if you got caught."

"You never reported it stolen. That car saved my life. I lived in it the first year after I ran away."

He nodded.

"How come you're no longer a parole officer?"

His dark eyes focused a little sharper, his jaw jutting out a little, his masculine lips tightening.

Oh, God. "Did you quit because of me?" Had she been that bad?

He backed away from her, to the window, and looked out. He said nothing.

"You did?" She stared.

He did a sexy, one-shouldered shrug. "Technically, I was let go."

She stared some more as she tried to make sense of that.

"Why? You were really good. You were the only decent person I met in the system. If anyone could have made me go straight, it was you. You just got me too late. I was… Look, nobody could've gotten through to me by that point. Why on earth would they let you go?"

He turned back to her, holding her gaze. "There was that letter."

For a long second, she had no idea what he was talking about. Then it clicked. "The email I sent?"

"Work emails are not private."

"But I was thanking you for all your help and apologizing for the car—"

And then it hit her.

Heat flushed her face. The email… *Oh, God.* At the end, in a fit of teenage drama, she'd confessed her undying love. She might have even mentioned that she would be saving her virginity for him.

She'd blocked that memory, apparently, until now. She cringed as she pushed to her feet and busied herself with packing up the first-aid kit. FBI agents didn't blush, she tried to remind herself, too late.

"I'm sorry," she said without looking at him. She couldn't just now.

She had a fair idea what had happened. He'd probably been accused of encouraging her teenage fancy. He hadn't. The opposite, if anything. He'd always tried to treat her as a big brother would, which used to frustrate the living daylights out of her.

"I'm really sorry," she said again, feeling it in the bottom of her soul.

"Don't worry about it. I found my place."

She didn't know what to say. She put away the white box and moved out to her kitchen to put a little distance between them. "Would you like a drink?"

"I better get going." But he stayed where he was and watched her for a long minute. "There was one thing I could never figure out. Why did you set fire to the house?"

The air got stuck in her lungs. "Your house burned down?"

Again, he waited awhile before he spoke. "Could have been an accident." He shook his head, then scratched his eyebrow as he thought. "I had the oil pan over to the side. You knocked a few things over when you drove the car off the metal ramp, come to think of it. Something might have thrown a spark."

She'd burned his house down.

She sank into the nearest chair as the stark truth hit her. "I ruined your life."

He gave a wry smile. "Don't be too hard on yourself."

For the first time in a long time, she had no idea what to say. He was armed. Why hadn't he shot her yet?

She wasn't about to ask him and give him any ideas.

For her, coming here, seeing Shep again meant…tying up some loose ends from her past. He'd been a good memory. She might have even looked forward to showing off to him a little… *look, I've made it,* that kind of thing.

She might have spent some extra time on her hair and makeup this morning. He'd pushed her away years ago. Now part of her wanted him to see what he'd missed and maybe even regret it.

She closed her eyes. What a fool she'd been.

All these years, he must have thought of her only as his worst nightmare.

His phone rang, breaking the silence, and he answered it. She was ridiculously grateful for the chance to gather herself.

He listened before he said, "Okay, I'll be right there."

"What is it?" she asked, still a little dazed by his revelations. "Did they find the Mustang?"

He slipped his phone back into his pocket. "Not yet. It's probably hidden somewhere in a garage right now. It belongs to a Doug Wagner, who doesn't seem to be home at the moment. Keith went out there. He got a list of Wagner's buddies. A neighbor said Wagner likes to hang out with them at The Yellow Armadillo."

"Which is?"

"A seedy bar in Pebble Creek. Known smuggler hangout." He shrugged. "But he wouldn't be out in public right now, after a hit. We're going to run down his friends and see if he's holed up with one of them or, at least, if one of them is holding the Mustang for him."

He held out his phone for her, with a mug shot on the screen. The man in the picture was average-looking— beady dark eyes, greasy hair, giant chin.

She'd seen only a little of the Mustang's driver, but enough to match him to the photo. She pushed to her feet. "That's him. I'm coming with you."

"No." He said it as if he meant it, in that stern, disapproving tone she knew only too well. "You just got shot. You're probably still tired from flying out here. And now you're injured. Stay and rest. Just take the rest of the day off, all right? Give your body a chance to recover."

She bristled for a moment but then, just this once, she decided to give in to him. A few hours of distance might be just what the both of them needed to put the past behind them. They needed to do that so they could move forward.

"I'm really sorry about before. Do you accept my apology?"

He nodded without having to think about it.

"I'm glad it all worked out for you in the end. It's good to see you doing well."

"You, too." It was a relief that she hadn't driven him to alcohol or something. "When I come into the office tomorrow morning, we'll start over. Could we do that?"

"It's a deal." He walked out the door with a brief nod at her, then closed it behind him.

She had to give it to him, he wasn't one to hold a grudge. She wasn't sure she could have been as understanding. She thought for a minute about their past, about where they were now, and tried to put things into perspective. *Think positive.*

She did that, and she also thought of something that would let her show Shep that she'd changed, that she wasn't the same person who'd nearly ruined his life, that she was good at what she did now.

The sudden need to prove herself to him took her by surprise.

When she'd received the assignment, she got a list of the team members and a one-page memo on each. She knew she would have to face Shep and she didn't really think she'd have any problem with it. She'd expected an awkward moment or two, maybe, but then they'd get over it.

Reality, however, turned out to be a lot more complicated.

She looked up the address of The Yellow Armadillo on the internet, then walked to her closet. Just because she'd agreed to stay away from the office for the rest of the day, it didn't mean she was done with investigating. She wasn't here on vacation. She wasn't here just to observe and evaluate the team.

She was here to help them achieve their objective.

She'd come prepared, brought undercover clothes in addition to her FBI suits. She pulled on blue jeans, cowboy boots, left the tank top and combed her hair out, then pushed a cowboy hat over her head. *Ready.* She would hang out at the bar, nurse a beer and get a feel for local activity.

Wagner was the key. The Coyote must have sent him to take out Jimmy, a loose end. Wagner could lead them straight to the Coyote, who could take them straight to the terrorists. They needed Wagner.

Her car was at the office, but The Yellow Armadillo was just a few blocks away. A chance to clear her head was more than welcome. And she could use the walk to get a better feel for Pebble Creek. She took the stairs, adding a little more to the exercise.

Her phone rang. Unknown number.

"Hey, it's Jamie. Shep said you got shot. How are you doing?"

Okay, that was weird. She wasn't used to family checking up on her. "Just a scratch. Not to worry."

"If you need anything—"

"I'm fine." As a rule, she handled her life on her own. She didn't depend on people.

Jamie paused for a second. "Okay. Just wanted to check in."

The day was hot but not unbearable as she hung up and walked out onto the street from the hotel lobby. She turned right after the bank and walked down the side street until she found the bar.

Its sun-faded, chipped sign hung over a reinforced steel door, every inch scuffed, crying for a paint job. The parking lot was half-empty. Still, considering that it was before noon, that didn't seem like bad business. But if the bar turned a profit, the owner sure didn't invest in appearances.

When she stepped inside, the smell of beer and unwashed bodies hit her. At least a dozen people were drinking and talking at the tables. Could be they'd been out on the border, smuggling all night, then came here to grab a drink before they went home to sleep. Their gazes followed her as she cozied up to the bar.

The bartender towered more than a foot over her, drying glasses. *Definitely a bruiser.*

"Howdy." He glanced at the bandage on her arm, but said nothing about it. The bar wasn't the kind of place where people would ask questions about something like that, apparently.

"Hey." She sat by one of the columns that extended from bar to ceiling, holding a dozen ratty ads for local services and whatever. That way, at least one side of her was protected. She scanned the short hallway in the back, could see a turn at the end that probably led to the office, then the back exit.

The bartender looked her over. "What's your pleasure, little lady?" He raised a bushy eyebrow. She didn't belong here and they both knew it.

She thought about a beer before lunch, and her stomach revolted. "Wouldn't mind starting with coffee."

He pushed a bowl of peanuts a few inches closer to her and turned to the coffee corner. He was back with her cup in two minutes, powdered creamer and sugar on the side. "You new in town?"

"Traveling through."

A waitress sailed by and winked at her. "Looking for your next heartache?"

Lilly gave a smile, hoping like anything that she hadn't already found it. "No, definitely not." Letting her teenage crush with Shep reemerge would be beyond stupid. "Nice town, though. Might stay awhile," she added, suddenly inspired by the bottom ad on the post that caught her eye. The bar band was looking for a new singer.

"If I can find a gig." She nodded toward the ad and tried not to think how many years it'd been since she'd been onstage. But hanging out at the bar wouldn't give her half the chance to snoop around as working here a few hours a night would. It'd make her an insider.

"You sing?" the waitress asked as she waited for her orders to be filled. She was in her early forties, a bottle blonde, slim, wearing a white T-shirt with the bar's logo on it and a short black skirt with an apron.

"Ain't much else I can do. I got just the voice the good Lord gave me." Lilly tried to sound country, as if she might just fit in.

The woman looked doubtful, but she said, "Come back tonight. Brian's the boss. He'll be holding tryouts."

"Thanks—"

"Mazie. And this one here's Shorty." She

snorted as she indicated the bartender with her head. He fairly towered over the both of them, busy with the beer tap.

"Lilly. I think I might just try for that gig."

Even if Shep was totally going to kill her for it.

Chapter Three

Night had fallen by the time Shep and Keith made their way into town and pulled up in front of The Yellow Armadillo, after a long and dusty shift on border patrol that netted them nothing whatsoever. Normally, they would have taken a break before going into the office in the morning. But as close as they were to D-day, they'd decided to snoop around the bar a little first.

Lilly's hotel was just up the road. Not that Shep planned on stopping by for a visit. He watched for an empty space in the parking lot. He had to drive around to find a spot.

"Looks like they do good business." Keith scanned the cars, then turned to Shep. "So, did Lilly Tanner really burn down your house and steal your car and all that?"

"Don't want to talk about it."

But Keith kept waiting.

Fine. "It was an accident."

"How does somebody steal a car by accident?"

"The fire was an accident. She needed the car and…" He shrugged. There was really no good way to explain. "She wanted to start over." He'd never really held a grudge. "She was a messed-up kid and with reason. She had rough beginnings."

"True that. Sold for drugs by her own parents. That's harsh. Can you imagine?"

"Not really." He'd grown up in a happy, loving family.

"That's why you never reported the car stolen?"

He parked the car and shut off the engine. "She was just turning eighteen—she would have gone to jail. Being locked up would have broken her. She'd always been special, always stood out. I didn't want to see her broken."

He was glad she'd turned out okay. He would be even gladder when she left again. He stopped for a second and turned to Keith. "And now we're done talking about her. She's only here for a few days. It's not important."

Keith flashed one of his quick grins. "Whatever you say."

The bar sat on a side street a little back from the main drag, among service-type businesses: dry cleaner's, key copying and photocopying, a car mechanic a little farther down. The road back here was narrower and darker, the streetlights smaller and not as fancy as Main Street's, no lone-star flags, no advertising posters on the poles.

Keith got out. "Hope Wagner is here."

Shep followed. "Or the guy who was with him at the shooting. Look for anyone with a damaged wrist."

They'd put out a call to the local hospitals, but none had a patient with a gunshot wound like that. He might have gone to one of the underground clinics that served illegal immigrants. If so, they'd have no way of finding him through the health-care system.

Music filtered out to the street through the front door as they walked up, the smell of stale air and beer hitting them as they stepped inside.

Mostly men filled the bar, very few women. It seemed like the kind of place where farmhands would go to get sloppy drunk at the end of the day. A scrawny cowboy wailed on the stage, a sad song about losing his girl. The clientele paid little attention to him.

Shep and Keith bellied up to the bar and flagged down two beers. They were dressed as rodeo cowboys. With all the cowboy shirts, jeans and cowboy boots surrounding them, they fit right in.

He didn't spot anyone suspicious at first glance, except a bookie in the far corner doing some business, probably taking bets on the rodeo that would start later in the week.

The bartender slid their beers in front of them. "In town to try your luck?"

"We're in it to win it." Keith gave an enthusiastic grin. "Hoping for a break in the weather. No fun trying to train in over hundred-degree heat."

The bartender nodded with sympathy. "Where you boys from?"

"Pennsylvania." Keith puffed his chest out a little.

The man gave a whoop of a laugh. "There ain't no rodeo in Pennsylvania." He shook his head as a pitying look came into his eyes.

"There sure is." Keith grinned. "There are crazy bastards everywhere." He managed to sound proud of it.

An older guy on Keith's other side toasted them with his beer. "Amen to that."

The bartender kept laughing as he walked away.

Shep didn't mind some mocking. Being considered the village idiot was the perfect cover.

He pretended to watch the band and the out-of-tune singer onstage while he continued checking out the customers. He looked for specific faces, not just something suspicious in general. That helped. If Doug Wagner or his partner showed up tonight, they could grab him, take him in and ask him who'd paid them to shoot Jimmy.

None of his buddies had given up his location. And Shep's team couldn't find the Mustang, either.

The sad cowboy onstage finished his song and stood awkwardly for a lackluster applause before lumbering off the stage. The band stayed and another singer came on. This was one was a woman.

And then some.

Next to Shep, Keith gave a soft whistle.

She wore cherry-red cowboy boots, a denim skirt that was so short it was barely legal and a light green tank top that looked familiar.

He leaned forward to see better. Those curves… He didn't want to be thinking what he was thinking. He had to be mistaken.

She stopped in front of the microphone with her hat pulled low over her eyes, her head bent. She hadn't sung a word yet, but already she held the crowd's attention, something the previous performer hadn't managed. Chins were hitting the tables all over. The men ogled her as if they were ready to devour her.

Then she looked up and flashed a dazzling smile that lit up the room. She had a face to match the body, for sure. A couple of men growled with appreciation. Others let out more wolf whistles.

"Hot damn." Even Keith couldn't keep quiet, his voice laden with reverence.

Shep came halfway to his feet then caught himself and dropped back down just before he would have blown his cover. "What in blazing hell is Lilly doing up there?" He hissed the words between his teeth.

But Keith was too dazzled to listen.

SHE LOCKED HER knees so they wouldn't shake. It'd been a long time since she'd sung onstage. And she'd never been a country singer. Lilly flashed another smile before she nodded to the three-man band behind her and started into a country ballad, similar to the one the singer before her had chosen.

She was one minute into it when she realized it wasn't going to work for her, not at a place like this. The sweet love song was something women would listen to in the car while driving to school to pick up their kids. The rough-and-tumble men who filled the bar weren't looking for sentimental, no matter how good the chords were.

Brian had been clear that he wanted a performance that hit the ball out of the park. Revenue was weak on band nights now that their lead singer had quit. He wanted some serious dough coming in. He wanted something that would bring people in early and make them stay until the closing bell.

She tried her best, putting all the heart she had into the song. Unfortunately, nobody was listening. A lot of the men were looking at the stage, but they were staring at her legs.

Since the audition was to be decided by applause…If the men kept staring instead of clapping when she finished, she was sunk.

Brian had asked for one song from each singer. She glanced at him as he sat up front, paging through a ledger book. He'd paid very little attention to the auditions so far. He certainly didn't look as if he was ready to offer her the job on the spot. She needed to get his attention and she needed to do it in a hurry. Her ballad was almost over.

Oh, what the hell, since when did she play things safe? As she sang the last note, she glanced back and winked at the band, then turned to the audience.

"I like country," she said and flashed a smile when a couple of men hooted in agreement, "but I'm a versatile kind of gal, so how about I show you a little bit of something else?"

A drunk shouted a few suggestions of what he'd like her to show him. The rest of the men laughed.

She had the lights in her eyes, so she could only make out the first row, but she knew the bar was packed. Tryouts for a new lead singer brought in some extra people, Mazie had told her just before Lilly came onstage. People liked the idea of getting a vote. Liked to check out fresh meat, too, probably.

Lilly took the ribbing in stride and tossed her cowboy hat into the audience, whipped her long hair and belted out the first line of the chorus to "I Love Rock 'n' Roll" at the top of her lungs.

There was a second of pause. This was the moment where she might get thrown off the stage. But nobody booed and the manager simply watched her.

Then the band picked up the song.

Relief flooded her as she went on singing, excitement filling her little by little, and she danced across the stage as she sang, suddenly feeling like a kid again, without any worldly possessions, just the road and her guitar. She sang her heart out like she used to, the old moves coming right back as she rocked the hell out of the place.

She'd already been thrown back to the past by seeing Shep, and now this finished the job. She felt a decade younger and couldn't say she didn't like it.

"Yee-ha!" someone shouted.

Boots slapped against the wood floor, the applause deafening when she finished, with a few marriage proposals thrown in, and the men demanding more.

She felt a surge of satisfaction and just plain pleasure. She'd worked so hard to make herself into something more, something serious, that she'd forgotten how good this had felt.

"You have a fun night, now!" she called out to acknowledge the support.

The manager was grinning at her, looking pleased as peaches.

She grinned back then ran backstage, passing the next act going up, another lanky cowboy who stared at her with a troubled look on his face. She set aside the buzz of adrenaline and turned her attention to her true purpose for being here: covert surveillance. She turned off the rock chick and turned on the FBI agent.

For the moment, she was alone backstage. The narrow hallway connected the main bar with the office and the kitchen that prepared a dozen food items—all well salted to keep the drinking at an optimum. Her attention settled on a closed door at the end on her other side. She'd seen that earlier, had wondered where it led. This could be her chance to investigate.

The next contestant started into a song on the stage, sounding unsure. He had a good voice, but it seemed that her performance had thrown him. He didn't seem to be able to find his footing.

Lilly tuned him out as she hurried over to the mystery door and tried the knob. Locked. Since she was pretty sure they were close to the outside wall and there was no upstairs above the bar, if the door hid stairs, they'd be going to a basement.

She had lock picks in her pocket. She reached for them, but footsteps behind her made her spin around. The music was so loud, she hadn't heard him in time, not until the man was right behind her.

Brian's face was expressionless as he watched her. He said nothing, waiting for her to speak first.

She flashed him her best smile. "Is this the staff bathroom? I think somebody's in there."

"No staff bathroom. We all use the one by the jukebox." He didn't volunteer any information on where this door led.

She could have asked, but didn't want to sound as if she was snooping. "So how did I look on your stage?" she asked instead. "Felt right—" she grinned "—I tell you that. Nice crowd, too. I sure could get used to it."

He measured her up. "We've never done anything but country." He paused. "You know, from anybody else, this might not have gone down as well. But you…" His gaze stalled on her breasts for a second. Then slid to her injury. "What happened to your arm?"

She shrugged. "An argument with my last drummer."

"You fit the harder music, I guess. Maybe it's time for a change here. Let's try it for a few weeks. When can you start?"

"As soon as possible." They needed to find Wagner, and so far the bar was their only lead. "When could I get back on that stage, do you think?"

"We do live music Fridays and Saturdays. So how about tomorrow?" He named a dollar amount per night.

She didn't argue with him. She couldn't risk him changing his mind. It was Thursday. Tomorrow and the day after would give her two full nights to snoop around here.

"I'm in. Thanks. I'll be here tomorrow." She moved to pass by him, but just as she did, she felt his hand patting her bottom.

Really?

Oh, man.

She could have put him on his back with a single move. But right now, going undercover at the Armadillo was more important. So she smiled as she turned and said, "Hey! There'll be none of that."

Brian raised his eyebrows, then shrugged after a second. "As long as you bring in money, it's all good," he said and simply watched as she walked away from him.

Would have been nice if that was the last word on the subject, but she didn't think it would go as easy as that. Still, she'd cross that bridge when she got to it. She was in, and for now that was all that counted.

She grabbed her bag from behind the bar, then headed for the back door. She wanted to get a good feel for the place inside and out. Supposedly it was a known smuggler hangout. Did Brian know? Was Wagner involved? Did anyone smuggle any contraband straight through here? Did anyone here know anything about the terrorists coming through? She had two days to find out.

She pushed the metal door open. Grabbing some fresh air after her performance shouldn't raise any suspicions.

She'd driven around the block before she'd shown up tonight to sing, so she knew the bar backed onto a narrow alley. She expected that she might run into a couple of smokers out there. But she didn't expect to run into Shep.

He was about to come in as she stepped out. He looked pretty steamed about something.

She pulled up short to keep from running into him. "What are you doing here?"

His eyes glinted with fury as he grabbed her by the arm and pulled her aside. The door clicked closed behind her. They were alone in the alley that led to a side street on their left and ended at a brick wall two stores down on their right.

"What are *you* doing here?" He was all decked out in cowboy gear. And looked hot in it, dammit. The shirt perfectly fit his wide shoulders, the jeans pretty nice on his long legs.

While part of her appreciated the view, he didn't look as if he appreciated anything about her at the moment. He looked mad enough to commit violence.

"Why are you here?" He snapped the question at her again.

"I'm going undercover." She kept her voice down even if there wasn't anyone else out there in the ten-or-so-feet-wide space between buildings.

"Like hell." He dragged her away from the door.

She went with him, but only because anybody could come out from the bar at any moment, and she didn't want them to hear the conversation. She didn't want to blow her cover before she had a chance to use it.

He finally stopped next to an empty Dumpster. "Gyrating around the stage like that. In that…skirt." His nostrils flared. "What were you thinking?"

"Listen—" She yanked at the skirt that had ridden up her legs from walking, revealing the winding tattoo on her inner thigh—an old mistake. "The bar is connected to smuggling. Through Doug Wagner, it's also connected to the Coyote. In all likelihood, the Coyote was the one who hired Wagner to take out Jimmy before the law could catch up with him. The Yellow Armadillo is a decent lead. It's worth checking out. Isn't that why you're here?"

Instead of congratulating her on her good work, he looked as if he was grinding his teeth.

She remembered his mad face. It was as if they were back in the past all over again. She'd hoped he would be more…impressed with her this time around. Not that she needed his validation. She glared right back. "What's your problem?"

"You." He spit out the word. "On a stage. Naked."

Oh, for heaven's sake. She was fully clothed. "I've done worse on the road."

His shoulders stiffened. "I don't want to know

about it." He drew in a ragged breath. "That shouldn't have happened. You shouldn't have run away. I should have found a way to stop you."

All he ever wanted was to save her somehow, back then and now, apparently. While all she'd ever wanted, at least back then, was for him to see her as a woman. "Nobody could have stopped me. And it wasn't bad. Nobody beat me like at some of the homes. I was my own person. I grew up. I turned out okay."

"Better than most runaways," he grudgingly agreed, then let several minutes pass before he asked, "Is this what you did after you left? Singing?"

"You expected a crime spree?"

A hint of a smile tugged at the corner of his lips. "It crossed my mind."

She shook her head. "Things could have easily gone that way. But for whatever reason, I decided to go in another direction." She allowed a hint of a smile of her own. "Maybe it was your good influence. Believe it or not, your car was the last thing I lifted. I tried odd jobs, but I figured out pretty soon that singing paid the best."

"And then?"

"When I found a steady gig, I finally made enough to rent a room. The landlady was all right. She offered me fifty bucks off the rent as long as I attended GED classes."

Pat had been the closest thing to a mother Lilly had ever known. Never judged her, had never gotten in her face about anything. She'd taken Lilly seriously and treated her like some-body instead of a problem. Shep had done that, but for some reason she hadn't been ready with Shep. Then she was suddenly ready with Pat. Maybe spending some time living in a car had made the difference.

Shep let his hand drop from her arm at last. "And then?"

"One of the GED teachers talked me into taking a few college classes in criminal law. I think to discourage me from getting too cozy with some of the shadier guys at the bar where I was singing. I thought, why not? It was an area where I had some experience." No one knew that better than Shep. She'd gone to him with an impressive juvie record.

He looked skeptical. "College grew on you?"

"You know? It did." She'd liked the challenge of it, the thought of doing something she'd never figured she could be capable of. "I even got a scholarship. And singing brought in enough money to pay the rest of my expenses. I didn't quit the bars until I got hired full-time by the police department. They paid me to do more college. Then I moved to the FBI eventually."

He took a second to take that all in. "Why aren't you married, raising two-point-five kids in the suburbs?"

"Who says I'm not?"

His eyes widened. "Are you?"

She waited a moment before she shook her head. "I'd rather do something I'm good at." And she had time. She wasn't yet thirty.

He frowned. "You can be anything you want to be—"

"And I can achieve anything I set my mind to." She finished his old mantra for him. She'd heard it a few dozen times, or a hundred. "Why aren't *you* doing the family thing?" The brief she had on him said he'd never been married.

"I'd rather do one thing and do it well."

"Live to work?"

He watched her. "You made it up the ranks pretty fast."

She grinned into the darkness. "Turns out I'm good at something other than criminal mischief."

"Yeah, like giving me a headache without half trying," he said, but he no longer sounded mad.

"I'm sorry. About the past. Again. I didn't mean to—" She didn't finish. Rehashing her sins wouldn't work in her favor. "The point is, having someone undercover here would be an asset to the team—"

Movement at the opening of the alley caught her eye. She was facing that way, while Shep faced toward the bar.

The dark shape that had appeared was walking toward them. Then he walked under the bare lightbulb hanging above a rusted back door of some other business, and she recognized him from the mug shot. Doug Wagner, the guy in the red Mustang who'd shot Jimmy.

He eyed them with suspicion as he came closer. There was only one thing a rodeo cowboy and a woman dressed like her would be doing in the back alley, and it wasn't having a serious conversation, she realized in a flash.

Shep had been half leaning against the brick wall. She shifted to push him fully against the wall and nestled her body against his.

"Lilly." He said her name in a strangled whisper. He still hadn't seen Wagner.

She nuzzled his neck. "Just play along for a minute," she whispered into his ear as she ran her hands up his chest. She didn't mean anything by it, but found herself distracted suddenly. *Okay. Nice.* He definitely wasn't lacking in the muscle department.

For a moment, he stood stiffly, then he probably heard the footsteps at last because he caught on and put his hands on her waist. And nuzzled her right back, setting the sensitive skin on her neck tingling.

God, it'd been a long time since a man had made anything of hers tingle. She'd been married to her job for too long, had taken too many back-to-back assignments lately. This felt nice. It made her miss…something she'd never really had.

Of course, he was all her teenage fantasies come true. And then some. The hard planes of his body fit perfectly against hers. He was all sexy, hot male.

"You smell like leather," she whispered to him.

"New boots, new belt."

"Huh." Okay, so her response could have been a shade more intelligent, but…

Shep Lewis had his hands on her!

She'd pictured this happening a few hundred times when she'd been seventeen, but reality was so much better. Thank God she was grown up and had moved on and all that. It would be a disaster if she let that old crush come back, considering Shep was one of the men she was supposed to be observing and reporting on.

His hands tightened on her waist and he pulled her even tighter against him as Wagner passed by them, then went inside.

Her breasts flattened against Shep's hard chest. Heat flashed through her.

But when he said, "Was that Doug Wagner?" his voice held no desire, only anger.

She sobered a little as he set her away from him.

His eyes narrowed. "Why the hell didn't we grab him?"

"Let's see who he talks to first. If Wagner doesn't pan out, there might be another lead here at the bar. As you said, it's a known smuggler hangout. I want to keep my cover. I want to be able to come back tomorrow and Saturday."

"Our goal for coming here was Wagner."

"What if whoever he gets his orders from is here? The higher up we get on the chain of command, the more likely we're to find actionable intel. Wagner might not know the Coyote's true identity. But the guy he reports to could have that."

Shep's expression was that of supreme annoyance, but he pulled out his phone. "I'll call the office. You go in and keep an eye on him."

So she went back inside, aggravated that their close encounter had affected her, while it had done nothing to Shep. Like back in the day—with her mooning after him, and him ignoring her. She was so not ever going back to that. She might have been lonely. He might have looked hotter than ever. But she had her pride, dammit.

She barely walked three steps down the hallway before she spotted Wagner, the sight of him distracting her from Shep. He was hurrying toward that closed door she'd checked out earlier. He had a key. He turned it in the lock and quickly disappeared.

She hurried after him but, of course, he'd locked the door behind him. She tried to listen, but the band was still playing, a woman was singing now, and she couldn't hear anything else. She glanced around and pulled her lock picks from her pocket. Hopefully, Brian wouldn't show up this time. How bad could her luck get?

Not too bad, as it turned out. The manager stayed out of sight. And she had the door unlocked in under thirty seconds.

A semidark staircase led down in front of her. *Bingo.* A basement. That certainly had potential if any nefarious activities were going on around here.

She left the door open a crack so when Shep came inside, he might get a clue as to where she'd disappeared. Then she started down, trying to listen if she could hear anyone talking down there.

Until she went around the turn in the stairs

and ran into a three-hundred-pound chunk of bad attitude, wearing sweat shorts, a black muscle shirt and a full gallon of sweat. Pockmarks covered his face, his eyes small and mean.

She smiled at him, and did her best to look harmless and clueless. "Sorry. I was looking for Brian."

Two beefy, hairy arms reached out to grab her. If the dark glare and snarl the man shot her was any indication, he wasn't particularly happy to see her there.

Chapter Four

"Up," the man said.

Lilly didn't argue, but backed away from him as soon as he let her go. "Sorry." She smiled again, even wider. "I'm brand-new. Don't actually start until tomorrow. I got the gig. Can you believe it?"

"Auditions are still going on."

She lifted her shoulder. "I suppose Brian wants to let everyone who showed up at least sing. He seems so nice," she lied cheerfully.

The guy didn't look touched. His hand hovered near his waist.

She was pretty sure he had a gun tucked into his waistband behind his back. She was unarmed and obviously so. Her skimpy clothes couldn't have hidden anything. There was no reason for him to escalate.

But if he did, at least she was higher up on the stairs than he, in a better position, and was trained in hand-to-hand combat. She could take him down if things came to that. But only if she had to. She'd much rather keep her cover.

She kept backing up, looking lost and apologetic.

He didn't go for the gun. Maybe he was buying her act. When they were at the top of the stairs, he waited until she was up and out, then closed the door in her face. She heard the lock turn.

Okay. That could have gone better. But it could have gone worse, too. Bottom line was, she needed to find a way to get back down to that basement so she could figure out what on earth was going on down there.

Shep, who was just coming in through the back door, caught her eye and raised a questioning eyebrow.

She hurried over and filled him in.

"You went down there? Alone?" He said the words between his teeth.

She smiled in case anyone was watching them. They could be seen from the bar. Plenty of people hung around waiting on Shorty for a drink.

"Next time, you tell me." Shep spit out the words. "You're here to observe and advise."

"And assist."

"Dammit, Lilly."

Since she didn't want to argue with him—or

be seen with him too much—she simply walked away. She meant to hang out at the bar for a while and talk to Shorty and the waitresses if she got a chance. But Shep came after her. They came out of the hallway into the main area.

"How big is the basement?" he asked right next to her, so only she would hear.

"I didn't get far enough to see."

"I'll try to get down there later."

"They keep the door locked."

"If you managed, so can I."

Of course, because *he* would have to do everything, Mr. Hot Stuff Commando. She couldn't possibly be enough. He was never going to forget what a screwup she'd been. She pressed her lips together and turned away from him, just in time to see Doug Wagner head for the door up front.

He must have come up from the basement and gone around the stage the other way.

Keith was about six yards behind him.

She gave a double take. *Keith?* Were they all here? Lilly scanned the tables but didn't see the rest of the team.

He nodded to Shep, then toward Wagner, who pushed through the front door and was out of sight the next second. Keith followed.

"You stay," Shep told her under his breath.

"We need to grab him before he disappears." Then he took off after them.

SHEP STEPPED OUTSIDE just in time to see Wagner walk to a white sedan parked at the end of the street and drive off. Keith was already at the beat-up pickup they used as their undercover car, on his cell phone, probably calling in the development. Shep caught up with him and jumped behind the wheel, then took off after Wagner.

Keith stayed in phone contact with the others. "Suspect heading south. We're two cars behind." He muted the phone before he turned to Shep. "How did it go with Lilly?"

"Fine."

"She's hot. I mean, like—man, did you see the way she moved up there? Those curves…"

Shep gave an annoyed grunt. Not only had he seen them, they'd been pressed against him in the alley, a sensation he wasn't about to forget anytime soon, unfortunately. But just because he couldn't forget the incident, it didn't mean he was going to share his feelings about it.

Keith made some more appreciative noises, keeping the phone on mute. "You sure you're not going to hook up with her?"

"Absolutely not."

"I wouldn't mind asking her out for a drink,"

the idiot went on. "She's here to work with us. No sense being rude to her."

Shep's fingers tightened on the steering wheel. He hated the idea of *anyone* asking Lilly anywhere. But she was a grown woman, entitled to her own decisions, so he stayed quiet.

Wagner turned off the main road and they followed. He stopped his sedan in front of an apartment building and got out.

The building had four levels, maybe a hundred apartments. Looked like a fairly new place, the siding clean and trim, the windows double paned. Pebble Creek was growing, adding some housing around the edges. The complex was one of a dozen like it that Shep had seen while driving around.

What was Wagner doing here? His official address was a trailer park across town. Who was he visiting? With a little luck, it would be a connection to the Coyote.

The man turned back to the sedan, reached into the back and pulled out a rifle. He left his car running as he walked away from it.

Shep watched as the man hurried into the building. "I don't like it."

"Definitely not a good sign," Keith said, then called in the address to the rest of the team, who were on their way.

Still, it'd be at least twenty minutes before

they got here. He had no time to wait for reinforcements. They had to take Wagner into
custody before he killed anybody else, or got
himself killed.

Shep checked his weapon. "I take the front,
you take the back."

They got out and ran toward the building,
then separated when they reached the steps.
Keith went around to see if there was a back
entrance. Shep pushed through the front door,
weapon in hand but down at his side, in case he
ran into civilians.

The main lobby stood empty—Mexican tile
floor, no trash, no graffiti, a decent middle-class
kind of place. The far wall held a hundred or so
mailboxes. Two pink kid bikes stood in a back
corner. Didn't seem like drug-dealer-lair territory.

He could hear footsteps on the floor above
him. That would be Wagner most likely. Shep
followed, keeping his gun ready. He stole up the
stairs silently, hugging the wall.

When knocking sounded from above, a sharp
rap on wood, he moved faster. Seemed as if nobody responded, because the knocking continued. Then he could hear some small noise from
below. Probably Keith coming in from the back.
Was there a back staircase? There should be. A

fire escape if nothing else. It'd be nice if they could corner Wagner.

Shep kept moving up. One flight of stairs to go. Just a few more steps. He looked right when he made it up all the way, and saw Wagner raise his rifle as the door he stood in front of inched open.

Shep raised his gun. "Drop your weapon!"

Wagner swung toward him just as the door slammed in his face. He squeezed off a shot at Shep, missed, then started running in the opposite direction down the hallway.

"Drop your weapon!" Shep ran after him.

Wagner squeezed off another shot.

Shep ducked, but he had nothing to duck behind for cover. He kept moving anyway, wishing he had his bulletproof vest. But since they were coming from the bar, dressed as rodeo cowboys, neither Keith nor he had any real protection.

Wagner reached the end of the hallway and turned.

Okay. Shep slowed. *Showdown.*

But instead of surrendering, the man squeezed off another shot, then slammed through the last door to his left.

Shep ran forward to the spot where the man had disappeared. Emergency fire exit. With any luck, Keith would be coming up and they'd have Wagner trapped between them.

He pushed the door open and inched forward carefully, kept his weapon raised in front, in case Wagner was waiting for him. But he saw no one, and judging from boots slapping on the steps above, Wagner was going to the next floor up in hopes of escaping instead of going down.

Shep ran after him. "Stop right there and throw down your weapon!" He needed to catch up to the bastard before an innocent civilian got in the middle of this.

And then someone did.

He heard screams, ran faster. Saw Wagner at last in the next turn. The man was holding his gun at two teenage girls who'd apparently snuck into the staircase for a smoke. They were fifteen, tops, dressed in summer skirts and flip-flops. They were white with fear, their eyes rapidly filling with tears as they whimpered, their half-smoked cigarettes having fallen at their feet.

Wagner's eyes darted back and forth as he tried to figure out his next step. "You stay back," he demanded from behind the girls.

"Listen—" Shep didn't get to finish.

One of the girls panicked and dashed forward, tumbling down the stairs, throwing herself at him, screaming, nearly knocking him off his feet. Her flailing arms knocked his weapon aside as she tried to get behind him to safety.

"Get down!" Shep pushed her out of the way,

doing his best to keep her from hurting herself, dammit.

Wagner used the momentary distraction, shoved the other girl down the steps, too, on top of Shep and tore off running once again.

The girls didn't seem to have any injuries worse than a scraped knee.

Shep called back to them as he ran up the stairs. "Get back into your apartment, lock the door. Call 911 if you need medical help." Then he turned his full attention to the man running from him and gave chase as if he meant it.

Three more floors before he reached the door to the roof. He wasn't even breathing hard. Every man on his team trained every single day. He could go a hell of a lot longer than this little sprint.

Once again, he went through the door carefully, gun first, and prepared to duck from fire, but no bullets came.

Chimney and vent stacks broke up the flat, long roof that radiated back the sun's heat, making the air shimmer above it. He had a flashback, for a second, to his days in the Iraqi desert. He shook that aside and pushed forward. When a shot finally did ring out, he rolled behind a vent stack.

"Cease fire!"

But bullets kept coming, pretty hard and

fast. Wagner had to be hiding behind one of the chimneys. Looked as if he'd decided to make his last stand here.

"Cease fire!" Shep rolled over into the cover of a chimney that provided more substantial protection, caught sight of another fire-stairs door on the far end of the building just as Keith ducked through it.

He signaled, pointing at the spot where the shots had come from so far. Keith nodded back and rushed forward, into cover of a vent stack.

Shep waited until he was in place, then rushed Wagner. While Wagner was focused on him, Keith took his shot and sent a bullet through the guy's right shoulder.

Wagner went down screaming.

"Stay down! Hands behind your head!" Shep reached him and kept his gun trained at him. "Stay down! Drop your weapon!"

Down in the parking lot, cars pulled in squealing. Keith glanced over the edge of the roof. "They're here."

Good. The rest of the team could help with cleanup and damage control. Especially since police sirens sounded in the distance. It'd be a full-on party soon. Maybe the girls had called in. Probably other residents had also reported the gunshots. The police would want explanations.

He slapped the cuffs on Wagner, grabbed him

by the elbow and pulled him up. The man was crying and yelling about his shoulder. The idiot could dish out violence, but it didn't look as if he could take much when the tables were turned.

"You have the right to remain silent." Keith Mirandized him before Shep had a chance.

Had to be done. The man needed to be put away. No sense in letting him slip through the cracks due to a technicality.

They took Wagner down, met with Ryder who was rushing up the stairs.

"Anyone else?" he asked. "I had the rest of the team spread out through the building."

Shep shook his head. "Just this one."

Ryder talked into his radio unit. "Shooter in custody. Coming down the south-end fire stairs. Withdraw from building." He ended the connection before he asked, "Any injuries?"

"Just him as far as I know." Shep glanced at the bleeding wound on Wagner's shoulder. "He'll live." But they'd have to take him to the hospital before they could interrogate him. "Local police can go through the building."

Bullets had flown, and they had the ability to go through wood and walls. Somebody could be lying bleeding in one of the apartments for all they knew.

Jamie and Mo walked Wagner downstairs

while Ryder haggled with the local cops over who should have the man in custody.

Shep caught Keith's attention and gestured back toward the building with his head as he backed toward the entrance. Keith followed him.

"I want to know who he came to take out," he said once they were inside. He didn't want the local cops to see them and get it into their heads to interfere.

They moved up the stairs together and took up position on either side of the door in question, then pulled their weapons.

Careful, Shep mouthed. Whoever was inside had been face-to-face with an assassin just minutes ago. He might start shooting and ask questions later.

Keith rapped on the door then pulled back into cover. "Customs and Border Protection. Open up."

Footsteps sounded inside. "There's a shooter in the building."

Not anymore, and the man would know that. His apartment was in the front, his windows overlooking the parking lot. He would have heard the cops arriving, would have looked and seen Wagner taken outside in cuffs.

Shep kept his focus on the door. "He's in custody. We need to talk to all the residents."

A long moment passed before the key turned

in the lock. Then a small gap appeared, only a sliver of the man's face visible.

Shep put on his most trustworthy look. "We need to come in and check the apartment, make sure there are no other attackers."

"There aren't."

"We have to check for ourselves. Are you armed, sir?"

"What the hell do you think? People are shooting up the damn place."

"Please, put your weapon down and step back from the door."

Seconds ticked by until the guy made up his mind and they heard the metal of his gun click on the tile floor, heard him move back.

Shep pushed in and kicked the weapon to Keith with the back of his boot.

The man was in his mid-fifties, nearly bald with a handlebar mustache. He was tanned, but not weather-beaten like most cowboys and ranch hands who worked outside. His mouth was pressed into an angry line. His right wrist was bandaged, bloodstains on the white gauze.

Shep's gaze flew back up to his face, his eyes narrowing. He hadn't gotten a good look at the trailer park, but this one could definitely be the guy who'd ridden shotgun with Wagner. The one who'd shot Lilly before Lilly shot his hand.

"What's your name?"

"Shane Rosci."

"All right, Shane. I'm going to check your place to be on the safe side. You stay where you are." Shep moved forward, farther into the apartment, while Keith stayed with the man.

The place was a one-bedroom efficiency, clothes on the floor, dirty dishes in the sink. Didn't look as if the half-open closet held any other clothes but his. Seemed as if he lived alone here.

Shep checked for other weapons and drugs, signs of any kind of illegal activity. He went back to the living room when he didn't find anything. Didn't mean the guy wasn't a user or a dealer. He could have flushed everything when he heard the police sirens.

Shep nodded toward the bandages. "What happened to your hand?"

"Burned it cooking."

"How do you know Doug Wagner?"

"Who?" Shane's eyes went a little too wide with supposed innocence.

"The man who came here to shoot you."

He looked away. "I don't know what you're talking about."

Shep shifted his weight, tired of playing games. "Then you don't mind going to the police station in the back of the car with him?"

The man took a step back, outrage flashing

across his face. "You can't arrest me. I haven't done anything."

"How about the murder of Jimmy Fishburn yesterday?"

The man paled, sweat forming on his forehead. "I didn't—"

"Are you involved in smuggling?"

"No. I'm an honest citizen. I swear. I work at the electronics store."

"What do you know about the Coyote?"

"Who?"

"Why did Doug Wagner come here today to shoot you?"

The bluster leaked out of the guy, his shoulders going down. "I owe him money."

"For what?"

The man's gaze darted from Shep to Keith then back as a look of misery came across his face. "I want to talk to my lawyer."

Keith stepped up to him. "You can call him from the car. We're taking you in for further questioning. Let's go." He herded the guy out of the apartment as the man loudly protested.

They got down to the parking lot in time to see Ryder drive away with Wagner. Apparently, he'd won the argument with the police. Then the deputy sheriff came into view, and Shep realized why the cops had backed off. As Jamie's girlfriend, Bree had some idea of what their team was doing here. She and Jamie had probably made some kind of a deal.

She came right over. "Everything okay?"

Shep put the man into the pickup. Keith moved over to the other side so the guy couldn't skip out that way.

"We're taking him over to the office." Wagner would be at the E.R. for a while with his shoulder, which meant they could have the interrogation room for Shane.

Bree raised a slim eyebrow. "I assume at one point I'm going to be updated on what's going on here?"

"That's not my decision. Sorry." If Jamie trusted her, so did he, but he wasn't the one setting the confidentiality level of the op.

She shook her head with a long-suffering look and waved them off.

Unfortunately, as it turned out an hour or so later, Shane had no knowledge of the Coyote. He owed money to Wagner for drugs. When he couldn't pay, Wagner insisted on his help with a job. Wagner had told him they were going to send a "message" to some guy. He'd said nobody would be at the trailer.

Shane had no idea they'd killed someone until he saw it on the morning news. He'd called Wagner in a panic, who then showed up to shoot him.

"I'm innocent here." He was sweating buckets now. "I'm as much a victim as that Jimmy guy was. I swear. I did nothing."

"You shot at me and my partner when we went after you," Shep reminded him. "You hit her, actually."

"You weren't in a cop car. How in hell was I supposed to know who you were? You can't spit around here without hitting a gangbanger. I thought you were maybe the guy whose stupid trailer we hit, all mad about it."

After leaning on him pretty hard for another hour, Shep was tempted to believe him. He called Bree to come pick him up. He'd be charged with Jimmy's murder and whatever could be proven on the drug angle with Wagner.

Once they'd left, Keith and Shep drove back to the office for their own cars so they could head back to their apartments for some shut-eye before their border shift started.

Their break passed pretty fast. Long before Shep was ready for it, they were on patrol duty. Didn't seem as if they ever really slept lately, just ran from one task to the other.

"Wouldn't have minded being in on the Wagner interrogation," he told Keith over the radio as they drove along the Rio Grande, each in their own SUV.

"They'll lean on him hard." Keith was a couple of miles ahead of him, out of sight.

Yes, they would. His team was the best of the best. Whatever the bastard had, they'd get it out of him. He thought about that as he scanned the area, taking advantage of the moonlight, switching to night-vision goggles when something moved and he needed to see better.

But they saw nothing all night other than deer and a couple of stray armadillos. Plenty of time to think about the op, and plenty of time to think about Lilly, unfortunately.

He hated the idea of her at The Yellow Armadillo, drunk ranch hands drooling all over her. He felt responsible for her. His first instinct was to protect her. Except their relationship now was completely different than when he'd been her parole officer.

In more than one way.

Why in hell did she have to throw herself into his arms in that back alley, dammit? Now he couldn't get the shape of her, the feel of her pressed against him, out of his mind.

She didn't want his protection. Too bad. She would have it anyway.

But other than for the purpose of saving her life, if it became necessary, he wasn't going to touch her again. Ever. Because it was wrong. And because—

The hell of the thing was, he wasn't sure if he could stop again once he started.

Chapter Five

Since Lilly got the gig, she was invited back on-stage to sing the last set.

The audience was pretty rowdy by then, The Yellow Armadillo still packed at close to two in the morning. Brian should be happy. The men certainly looked as if they'd had plenty to drink. The cash register should be close to bursting.

She watched her inebriated audience as she sang, searching for any possible illegal activity. She tried to figure out who the regulars were, and kept an eye on who went out to the back hallway that led to the basement, how long they stayed, if they returned.

She wished she could afford risking another try at that basement door after she sang the last song, but she couldn't. She couldn't get caught twice in the same evening. She got the gig, would have access to the bar again tomorrow. That was sufficient progress for her first day.

She wondered how Shep and Keith had made

out with Wagner. Not that either of them had thought to call and let her know.

She finished her last song to enthusiastic applause, gave a smile and a quick bow before running off the stage, ignoring the catcalls. She thanked the band as they came off the stage behind her, bringing some of their instruments and going back for the rest.

She smiled at the keyboard player, Sam. "Can I give you a hand?"

The band was here two nights a week. They must have seen a thing or two. She could do worse than getting friendly with them.

The fiftysomething man grinned at her. "Sure."

"Is it always like this?" she asked as she helped him take apart the keyboard stand.

"On a good night."

"And on a bad?"

"Fistfights. Or some idiot will pull a gun."

She tried to look scandalized. "I hope the cops don't shut us down on a night when I'm singing. I really need the money."

Sam shrugged. "Brian doesn't call the cops. He has people to deal with guys who get out of hand. Shorty's got a mother of a rifle behind the bar."

She'd bet he did. And then there was the meat mountain if Shorty needed backup.

"You guys make a pretty good band." A compliment could go a long way toward establishing goodwill, and maybe a connection.

"You're not bad yourself," he said as he walked out back with his equipment.

The back door stood propped open for the band, letting in some fresh air. One of his buddies had pulled the band's van up to the back door. The alleyway was just wide enough to allow a single vehicle.

She helped them load. It gave her another few minutes to hang out with them. Then they were done and getting into the cab. "Hey, thanks. See you tomorrow night."

"You bet."

The main area of the bar was mostly cleared out by the time she went back in. She sidled up to the bar and asked for some ice water. She was hot and sweaty from jumping around onstage, but she saved icy drinks for when she was done. Anything cold constricted her throat and made singing more difficult.

Shorty put a glass of ice water in front of her. He gave a lopsided smile. "Damn if you didn't make me feel twenty years younger."

She narrowed her eyes as she watched him. "Are you trying to tell me you're over twenty?"

He gave a booming laugh. "You're all right for a drifter, you know that?"

"I prefer to think of myself as a woman of the world."

He snorted.

She drank. "How long have you been working at The Armadillo?"

He shook his head. "Think I might have been born behind this bar. Mama used to waitress here."

"You like working for Brian?" she asked carefully, glancing at the jumble of ads on the column by the bar, pretending that the question wasn't important, just something to say.

Shorty shrugged as he put up the clean glasses. "Boss man's the boss man. They come and go every couple of years."

No big surprise there. Bars and restaurants changed hands frequently.

She grinned. "I'm just glad he likes the way I sing." She made sure she sounded super enthusiastic, as if this was her big break.

The meat mountain she'd encountered in the basement slogged by, nodded at Shorty. "Wagner came back yet?"

"Haven't seen him."

Lilly waited until the man walked away before she asked, "Who is he?" He'd been down in the basement with Wagner. Maybe he was Wagner's connection to the Coyote.

Shorty turned back to his work. "He delivers the booze for Brian," he said over his shoulder.

A name would have been better, something Lilly could have run through the database back at the office. But she didn't ask. Not tonight. Asking too many questions would jeopardize her cover.

She hung around until the very end, observing the dynamics among the staff, noting who was friends with whom, who goofed off, who took their job seriously. Mostly everyone just went about their job. They all looked tired. As hard as she watched, she didn't see anything suspicious.

Yet she felt that she wasn't wrong about the place. Something was going on here, something not quite on the up-and-up. She wished she had more time to get to the bottom of it.

Tomorrow night she would be back to sing a full set. She would get meat mountain's name. And she would find a way to get down into that basement.

Brian emerged from his office and called to Shorty as he strode to the front door. "Don't forget to put up the notice."

Shorty shook out the dishcloth. "I'll do it as soon as I'm done with the glasses."

"Thanks." The manager said good-night to

the staff, then left for the night, leaving them to finish the work.

Lilly swallowed the last of her drink and pushed her glass to the dirty pile. "What notice?"

"We'll be closed on the first. Need to have some electric work done. Boss wants to put in a bigger air conditioner, but first we have to upgrade the wiring. There'll be people here working on that. We won't have power most of the day."

"That's tough." She glanced at the air-conditioning system, which looked fine to her and worked okay tonight. "Nobody likes to lose a day's income. Hope the electrician works fast." But her mind was turning the information this way and that, trying to see if it might fit the rest of the puzzle pieces in her head.

The bar would be closed on the first of October. The day when those terrorists were to sneak across the border.

She didn't believe in coincidences.

SHEP DIDN'T CALL Ryder until he got off his shift Friday morning. He'd wanted to give the guys at the office time to work on Wagner.

"Did he talk?"

"Idiots like him, they're only big boys while they have their big guns. Once we had him in interrogation and convinced him of the gravity of his situation, he would have given up his mother for a deal."

"His mother is the Coyote?"

"Funny guy," Ryder groused on the other end, probably rolling his eyes. "Anyway, the order to kill Jimmy came through a man at The Yellow Armadillo. A guy who goes by the name Tank. Know him?"

"I'll find him. What else?"

"Wagner got ten grand for the hit, also through Tank."

"What was he doing at the bar last night?"

"He says he just went for a drink. Maybe he needed to fortify himself before the hit."

Shep chewed on that for a minute before saying, "Lilly will be at the bar tonight."

Ryder grunted on the other end. "I'm not any happier about that than you are. She called to let me know about her undercover stint. Next time she does something like this, she better clear it with me first."

She better not ever do anything like this again.

"She said the bar will be closed on the first. Supposedly they're upgrading their wiring," Ryder said.

"Interesting timing."

"That's what I thought. The bar might be first stop for the men coming across the border.

Come across, lie low for a day to rest, move up north from there. That basement you were talking about has potential. Lilly wants to look into it."

"I want to switch shifts so I can keep an eye on her."

"Jamie asked, too."

"Keith and I already have a cover established there."

"Fine." Ryder paused. "You go to the bar. But not Keith. We have a new gang-related lead out of San Antonio that might take us to the Coyote. I want Keith to be working that angle. But if you want to spend some time looking around The Yellow Armadillo, we can set that up." He hesitated for a second. "Just don't let yourself get distracted."

"It's not like that."

"Good. That's what I wanted to hear."

Shep drove back to his apartment for some sleep after they hung up, then spent a couple of hours at the office before heading to the bar that evening. The band started playing at eight.

He went early to get a table that would give him a good view of most of the bar and the stage, and the opening to the hallway that led to the basement and the exit door to the alley. He ordered a beer and nursed it slowly as he observed the people around him and listened in on conversations.

When the bar began to fill up and he could do it without drawing attention, he headed to the back hallway. He wanted to check out the basement Lilly had discovered. Finding a way down there and figuring out Tank's identity was his mission for the evening.

The band was coming in from the back, carrying their equipment through the hallway and up to the stage.

Shep moved to the basement door, as if waiting for someone, blocked the lock with his body, and tried to pick it behind his back as people hustled around with microphone stands and extension cords, drums and whatever.

A small click told him he was getting somewhere. Once the door was open, he'd wait for a moment when the hallway was empty, then he'd quickly pull in there. Nobody paid much attention to him. The band members were focused on their equipment and hurrying with the setup, which would work in his favor.

But before he could have popped the lock, footsteps drummed behind him and the door opened, whacking him in the back.

He stepped aside. "Easy there."

The young guy who came up shot a dark look at him. He had tattoos running up both arms, his shirt covered in dust. Looked as if he'd been working hard. Doing what?

"Tank down there?" Shep improvised.

The kid had been reaching back to close the door, but the question stopped him. He stuck his pointy chin out, trying to look tough. "Whatcha want with him?"

Shep kept his face impassive. "That's my business, ain't it? Wagner said he'd be here."

The kid shrugged then jerked his head toward the stairs. "Lock the door behind you."

Shep didn't. He wasn't about to close his only avenue of escape, not when he had no idea what he was walking into. He might need to come back up this way in a hurry.

The stairs were badly lit. He couldn't have seen down all the way anyway, since there was a turn in the staircase. He plodded down, going as if he had every right to be there. No sense in being tentative and looking as if he was sneaking around.

The basement room he reached was maybe twenty by twenty, four doors leading into other rooms, bare cement brick walls, cracked cement floor. Open boxes of booze stood everywhere. He couldn't see anyone, but he could hear people talking in one of the rooms to his left.

"Anybody who'd put a grand on that kid is an idiot. He's a greenhorn."

"He's been competing all year. Winning."

"Where? Podunk, New Mexico? He ain't never ridden in a rodeo as big as this. There're a hell of a lot more serious riders here. Kid won't stack up. You put any money on him, you'll be losin' it."

While he had the chance, Shep passed by the nearest shelf and pressed a bug on the bottom of it, out of sight. He stepped away just in time. Another skinny, tattooed guy was coming from the back room, this one bald with a row of metal in his left ear.

The kid stopped in his tracks. "Who the hell are you?"

"Howdy." Shep stepped forward, then cleared his throat as if he was nervous. "Someone said I could find Tank down here."

At that, a mountain of a man appeared, his eyes narrowing as he looked Shep over. Okay, that had to be Tank. He looked as if he could take a guy out just by sitting on him.

He was breathing a little hard, probably from whatever they were doing in the back. His small eyes narrowed in his pockmarked face. "What the hell are you doing here?"

Shep glanced at the tattooed kid, then back to Tank. The two must have gone to the same charm school. "Can we talk someplace private?"

The mountain jerked his head at the kid,

and the kid retreated into the back room he'd come from.

Tank stayed where he stood. "Talk."

Shep shifted his weight onto one foot and tried to look sheepish. Not an easy task for someone who was commando to the core. He didn't have much practice. But maybe he could pull it off in the dim light. "I'm here for the rodeo. Thing is, I really wanna win it. I'm hoping you could help me."

Tank glared. "Who the hell told you that?"

"Guy I had a beer with here yesterday. Wagner."

"Can't keep his mouth shut now? What the hell?"

"I need this, man." Shep shifted his weight again. "I'm not from around here. I don't know who to ask. If you could help…"

Tank raised an eyebrow, waited a couple of seconds. "You got money?"

Shep dug into his pocket and came up with a roll of twenties. He'd come prepared.

The man still looked more aggravated than excited with the new business. "You stay here."

He went back into the room he'd come from. A couple of minutes passed before he returned with a Ziploc bag of white pills, six of them. Probably performance-enhancing drugs. Shep wasn't about to ask questions. He needed to look as if he did this all the time.

He looked at the pills. "That'd be perfect. Just what I need."

The lab could figure out what they were. If they couldn't get Tank on smuggling, at least they could get him on the drugs. The man named his price and Shep paid it.

"Thanks." He held the bag as if the pills were made of gold at the very least, careful not to put his fingers where Tank's had been. He didn't want to damage the fingerprints. "I really appreciate this."

But Tank was already walking away from him. "It's a onetime deal. I don't know you, and you don't know me. Don't let me see you down here again."

LILLY WAS WALKING by the manager's office, on her way to the stage, psyching herself up for her performance, telling herself she could still do this, when Brian called her in.

He was sprawled in his chair behind the desk as he looked her over. "You dressed like a nun for a reason? Them cowboys like a little skin."

She wore bloodred, spiked heels, a skintight black leather skirt that barely covered her behind. It showed off the winding tattoo on her inner thigh—something she'd gotten to gain

Shep's attention, back in the day, which she did, but not in a good way. He hadn't thought it'd made her a woman. He'd been angry about it.

Brian, on the other hand, seemed to appreciate the art, judging by the way his gaze lingered on the spot. Then slowly slid higher, to the glittery shirt that was pretty much molded to her torso.

"No problem." She smiled, even if she was gritting her teeth, and undid another button on top. The lace edge of her red bra was showing now. That better be enough. She scanned his desk to see if he had any paperwork out that might give a clue to his illegal activities or a possible link to the Coyote, but all she could see were utility bills.

He kept ogling her with a lecherous grin. "A little more skin wouldn't hurt."

But breaking your face would. She kept on smiling as she shoved up the shirt enough so her belly button showed. At the same time, she scanned the windowless office and noted the file cabinets. Would Brian keep anything incriminating here? Probably not. He was slimy, but she didn't think he was stupid.

He wasn't subtle, either. "A little more?" He pushed.

"I think I'm okay. Band is waiting." She walked away before she could have clocked him.

While Brian approved of her way too much, Shep was the opposite. He thoroughly disapproved of her gig here. Thank God he wouldn't be here tonight to glower at her. As far as she knew, he was on border duty.

She ran up onstage and tore into a song, sang a couple of rock ballads to ease the crowd into the mood, took it easy with the jumping around, since she couldn't afford to pop a button. Her shirt barely concealed her bra as it was. She picked up volume and energy as she went on, and by the time the first set was finished, people were singing along with her, in a drunken-cowboy choir.

Since the lights were in her eyes, she couldn't observe the audience as well as she would have liked, except for the first two rows of tables. She would just have to use her breaks and after-hours staff time to do her spying.

By the time she was finished with the first set, she had sweat rolling down her back. The bar had plenty of air-conditioning, but it was still hot under the lights. She grabbed her bag from behind the bar and something to drink then walked back to the bathroom to throw some cold water on her face—reviving herself almost as good as coffee would have.

It'd been a long day. She'd spent the morning and afternoon working at the office before coming here.

She touched up her makeup before squeezing into a stall and switching tops, yanking on a black lace tube top, tight and strapless, she'd brought for her second set. Brian ought to be happy with that.

Except he wasn't. She ran into him on her way out.

"Overdressed again?" His sticky gaze slid down the length of her body.

She didn't want to lose the gig so, she kept a smile on. "Can't go up onstage in just a bra."

"Why not?" He stepped closer, tilted his head as his gaze settled on her breasts. "Maybe a studded leather one. I guess I could spring for the cost."

He reached out, dragged a finger up the middle of her belly, between her breasts, to her chin and lifted her head. "You give a good show. No reason why you couldn't give even better. Maybe I'll throw in a little bonus." He winked at her.

She couldn't remember the last time she wanted to deck a guy so badly. But before she could have lost her cool and her undercover position, someone grabbed her hand from behind, spun her around, and the next second she was brought up hard against Shep's wide chest.

"Babe." He flashed a sultry grin. "You were hot up there." And then he claimed her lips.

For about a half a second she tried to figure out what was going on, then gave in to the firm pressure of his mouth. *Oh, man.* So, soooo much better than what she'd imagined back in the day. *Wow.*

She couldn't not notice how perfectly they fit together, how great he smelled, how strong the arms that held her were. He was pretty damn good, playing the sexy cowboy. She so wasn't going to fall for it.

But as much as she told herself that, she was still a little dizzy by the time he let her go.

Brian cleared his throat. "Boyfriend?" He was watching them tight-lipped, his forehead pulled into a displeased frown.

Shep tipped his hat. "It's still new, but I tell you, I'm over the moon about this little lady. Luckiest day of my life was when I walked in here."

He stood a full head taller than Brian, all muscle, while the manager was made up mostly of beer weight as far as she could tell. Brian must have noted the difference between them, too, and correctly assessed his chances if they came to blows over her. He walked away with an aggravated grunt.

She pulled back enough from Shep so she could think again. "Now what?"

"Now we play out what we started." He dragged her to an empty table, yanked her down onto his lap and put a protective hand on her waist. He didn't look around, but they both knew people took notice that he'd made his claim on her.

"You're welcome," he said under his breath.

He had a smile on his face for whoever was watching, but she could feel the tension in his muscles. More disconcertingly, she could also feel the heat of his palm on the bare skin of her lower back.

"I didn't need your help," she let him know in a whisper. "Maybe I was flirting with him as part of my cover."

The fake smile slid off his face. "Don't."

"You're not the boss of me." She would have said more, but the band was back onstage waiting on her.

She began to rise, but Shep pulled her back down and kissed her again. It really was a chaste kiss, like the first, just his lips resting against hers, and the slightest pressure. But his masculine scent enveloped her, his muscles flexing under her fingers as she reached up to hold on to his arms, their bodies pressing together.

His lips were warm and firm and they...lingered. It was the lingering that did her in, the wondering whether he would go further, the tension in his body that said he wanted to. Or maybe she was reading things into a theatrical gesture.

That would be pitiful on her part. And she refused to be pitiful about Shep Lewis ever again. She pulled away and looked him in the eye. "What was that for?" she asked to clarify things. "Brian is back in his office."

"To let these other yahoos know that you're off-limits."

Right. He was acting a part. The both of them were. She had to make sure she didn't forget that. She had no intention of walking down the long road that led to heartache.

"I'm going to make sure you're safe," he promised.

"No."

"I couldn't keep you safe when I should have. I should have never let you run away."

"I would have liked to have seen you try to stop me."

"I didn't try very hard," he admitted. "I wasn't sure if the system was the best place for you."

"It wasn't."

"Had to be better than the streets."

"I made it. Chill."

"I'm going to have your back this time," he insisted stubbornly.

That protection wasn't what she wanted from him—then or now—seemed to completely escape him, she thought, frustration tightening her muscles as she walked away.

Chapter Six

Shep went to get another beer while Lilly did her rock-star act onstage, mesmerizing the audience. He stayed at the bar. It was the easiest way to be close enough to people to overhear conversations, to keep an eye on the staff and who they interacted with and how.

Shorty, the bartender, put a beer in front of him. "Weren't there two of you yesterday? Where's your buddy?"

"Twisted an ankle in training."

"Bulls are more polite in Pennsylvania, eh?" He laughed, cracking himself up.

Shep laughed with him.

An older cowboy next to him was leaning against the bar, facing the stage. He pushed up his cowboy hat with his index finger. "That's one fine filly up there."

"All mine," Shep said and puffed his chest out, acting very pleased with himself.

The cowboy grinned, patting his mustache. "If you can hang on to her."

Shep flashed him a cocky look, as if he didn't have a doubt in the world. But the truth was he didn't want to hang on to Lilly. Hanging on to her was doing things to him. Uncomfortable things.

He'd acted on the spur of the moment when he'd kissed her, because he hadn't been sure which one of them would knock the manager's head into the wall first. Seeing the oily bastard's hands on her snapped something inside him. It was a miracle he'd been able to play it as cool as he had.

The kiss had seemed the perfect way to defuse the situation while allowing both of them to keep their covers. The second time, he did it to make sure all those horny cowhands, too, would know she was spoken for.

He hadn't meant to enjoy it.

It was wrong to enjoy it.

No way was he going to do it again. Unless he absolutely *had* to kiss her to keep their cover. But he would hate it next time. For sure.

He drew a long swallow as his new undercover girlfriend danced across the stage. No reason why Jamie would have to find out about this latest turn of events. Or Mitch Mendoza for that matter. Thank God Mitch was on an op in South America at the moment.

Shep turned his attention elsewhere and scanned the drooling men. He wasn't going to discover anything by staring at her like the rest of the idiots.

Brian was nowhere to be seen. Tank, if he was still here, was down in the basement. He would have liked the guy's full name so he could run him through the system. As it was, he'd have to scan mug shots on the computer at the office in his free time, in the hopes that he'd stumble on the guy by chance.

He drained his beer and got up, walked outside as if for a smoke, leaned against his car in the parking lot and pulled out his phone, set it to the right channel. Out here, he could hear everything the bug was transmitting from the bar's basement. Inside, it'd been too loud to monitor that, but everything got recorded, so he could go over it later tonight. Right now, all he wanted to do was check in, see if Tank was still down there.

"Is that the last crate?" somebody asked. Enough of the music upstairs filtered down to make the words difficult to make out, let alone identify the speaker.

Still, to Shep, it kind of sounded as if it might have been Tank.

"Yeah" came the response.

"You brought the empty bottles down?"

"Right here."

"All right, boys, let's fill 'em up, then."

Sounded as if they were working with some homemade booze, maybe tequila distilled on the other side of the border, smuggled up here and sold as the real deal. Whenever a genuine bottle of booze ran out, it would be refilled with the cheaper stuff, again and again. But sold at regular prices, it would increase Brian's profits twofold, at least.

Another thing Tank could be put away for, and hopefully the manager, too. That cheered Shep a little. He'd hated Brian's hands on Lilly.

He listened some more, hoping either Doug Wagner's or the Coyote's name would come up. They didn't. The good old boys in the basement only talked about booze and women. They had very limited focus as far as that went.

After a few minutes, he turned off the phone and walked inside to check on Lilly.

He wondered what her FBI colleagues would say if they could see her now. The old cowboy had been right. She was plenty hot up on that stage in that lacy black tube top and sky-high heels. She kept the crowd going.

She sang another set, freshened up, then came

to have a drink with him. Water for her. He slowly nursed another beer.

"Looks like you're having fun up there," he said.

"No point in singing to be miserable."

She had a point. "Do you have to wear so… little?"

She laughed. "Brian wants me in less."

One of these days, Brian would get what was coming to him, he thought morosely.

When she stood to go back up onstage, he figured he better not kiss her again, so he just patted her behind playfully. For appearance's sake.

Another thing he would have to learn not to enjoy, because on the first run he enjoyed it way too much, unfortunately. He wondered if he could convincingly play her boyfriend without touching her.

Not likely. No man could keep his hands off a woman like her if she belonged to him.

Halfway through the set, he got up again. This time he walked out through the back door. If the basement had any windows, he hadn't seen them from the front. He wanted to check in the back.

Two ranch hands and a tattooed young kid from the basement were leaning against the wall smoking, listening to the music filtering through the door, discussing rodeo horses. Shep stood a distance away from them, turned so he could examine the back side of the building. Old brick, no windows on the main level or the basement. The building was probably built way before there were building codes requiring outside basement exits.

He pulled the pack of smokes he kept as a prop in his shirt pocket, took a cigarette and shoved it between his lips, but didn't light it.

A couple of other places had back doors to the alley, a pizza shop on one side, dry cleaner's on the other, a few more down the row. They all had security cameras above their doors, except for The Yellow Armadillo.

With tens of thousands of dollars' worth of liquor behind the bar, and more in the basement, their lack of concern over security was interesting. Unless they wanted no recording of who came and went through the back.

The light above the door was maybe twenty watts, not illuminating a hell of a lot. He wouldn't mind coming back here later tonight, after the bar was closed and everyone had left, to gain entry to that basement and see what Tank was hiding in those back rooms. He shifted on his feet.

The tattooed kid looked his way. "You need a light?"

Shep spit the cigarette to the ground and

crushed it under his heel. "Trying to quit. Thanks anyway."

"Good luck with that," the kid said. "I try at least once a year."

The ranch hands gave him sympathetic nods.

"You here for the rodeo?" one of them asked.

"You bet. Shep," he said, introducing himself. "Down from Pennsylvania. You?"

"Brandon here might try." One of the ranch hands nodded toward the skinny, tattooed guy.

That was good. Shep needed names. "How about you two?"

"Nah, Nick has a bad back. I got a bad horse." The man gave a sour laugh.

"I hear you." Shep shook his head. "Some days I think mine is the devil's spawn."

Nick gave a rueful laugh. "I had one like that. Almost broke my neck."

Shep gestured toward the bar's back door with his head. "So this place okay? My girl is singing."

"New chick?" Brandon asked. "Best keep an eye on her. Crowd can get rowdy."

He nodded. "How about the manager? Better pay her. Last gig she had, they stiffed her more weekends than not."

"Brian's cool. He don't mind paying under the table, either. Save some on taxes, if she's interested."

The manager sounded as if he didn't mind

breaking any number of laws whatsoever. Could be Tank reported to the Coyote, could be he reported to Brian. What if Brian was the direct link?

Something they had to figure out in a hurry.

THEY DID MAKE some progress with Tank. Shep put a rush order on the prints and they got the results back early the next afternoon.

"Zeb Miller, with a rap sheet as long as the Rio Grande," the lab tech said on the other end of the line and sent the file over.

Shep took it into Ryder's office.

"Wish we had time to follow him for a while, see who he meets up with." Ryder shook his head as he looked over the man's impressive list of offenses. "But we just don't. Why don't you go pick him up? Let's see if we can crack him."

They had to try—didn't really have a choice.

But Tank wasn't at the address listed as his rental and couldn't be tracked down, not even with an APB on his vehicle. Worse, that night when Shep went back to The Yellow Armadillo, Tank didn't seem to be there, either.

Maybe he had some sixth sense and got spooked. Or maybe he was on a run across the border and he'd be back later.

Shep settled in to watch the show. Mostly he watched the audience, keeping an especially close eye on Brian, who seemed to keep to his office tonight. There was no movement in the back hallway, nobody coming and going from the basement.

Lilly put on a hell of a show, once again. And as bad as watching her dance across the stage half-naked was, the breaks were worse. He thought he'd jump out of his skin every time she sat on his lap.

LILLY CHANGED AGAIN during her last break and finished her bottle of water as she walked over to Brian's office, trying to make progress in her investigation. She flashed a smile as if his groping had already been forgotten.

"I hate to ask for favors on my first night, but..." She winced. "I could really use a dressing room. I like changing between sets. Do you think it would be possible to find me a small place that's private?"

He looked a lot less excited about her now that Shep was in the picture. He barely looked up from his paperwork. "People always used the bathroom before. That's all we got. This ain't no fancy place."

"It doesn't have to be fancy. Last place I worked at let me use a storage room. How about a quiet corner down in the basement?"

He did look up at that and shook his head. "If you want, you can change in my office."

With him right there, no doubt. "You got glass in your door," she pointed out.

"The better to keep an eye on people coming and going."

She raised a teasing eyebrow. "You don't trust your staff?"

"I don't trust anyone."

His cell phone rang and he picked it up, pointed at the door for her to close it. She did, then meandered toward the basement door, but just as she could have tried the lock, Brandon came down the hall, so she stepped away.

He flashed her an unhappy look, unlocked the door and went through. She could hear him lock it behind him.

Great.

She pulled out her cell phone to check the time. She had five more minutes before her next set. She couldn't go downstairs now. And she better clear out before Brandon came back. She didn't want him to think she was loitering for a reason and say something to Brian.

She didn't want to go sit by the bar. If she stood alone, guys hit on her. If she went to sit with Shep at his table, he'd feel the need to act like her boyfriend and she wasn't sure how much more of that she could take tonight.

She walked up front, grabbed another bottle of water, then walked outside through the front door for some fresh air. The smokers usually hung out in the back alley, so the front was nice and quiet.

The street was mostly deserted at one in the morning, the row of small shops closed, but not darkened. She glanced down the rainbow of neon lights over the entrances. She was used to big-city lights in D.C., and this was nowhere like that, yet small Texas towns did have their own charm, she thought.

Movement at the car shop on the corner caught her eye. She couldn't see at first what exactly was going on. The repair shop didn't have their lights on like the stores. It was almost time for her to go back in, but on an impulse, she stayed and waited another minute.

There was that movement again. And when she looked more carefully, she could see a man coming from the repair shop carrying a box and watched as he put it into the back of a black pickup. A passing car illuminated him for a second. *Brandon.*

She pulled into the shadows so she wouldn't be seen if he looked this way.

It was definitely him—the same height, width, the same lumbering movement. How on earth had he gotten over there?

Only one explanation came to mind. The Yellow Armadillo had a tunnel, some kind of underground connection to the car shop. They definitely needed to find a way down there.

Music filtered through the door as the band inside began to play. She hurried back in.

She didn't have a chance to catch Shep on her way to the stage. He was talking to some guys up by the bar. But as soon as her last set was done, she searched him out in the dispersing crowd so she could tell him her theory about a tunnel.

"We have to know for sure what's going on in the basement. I want to go down there. Tonight," she clarified.

They stopped next to his pickup after walking out together. "Let the team handle it," he said.

"We're here right now. The last stragglers will be gone in ten minutes. No better time than the present. There's a twenty-four-hour convenience store on the other side of the corner, past the mechanic. We could pretend to be heading there to pick up something."

He looked down the street, then back at her. "Okay." And then he reached out and wrapped his arm around her.

Oh, man, was that necessary? Him touching her unsettled her every single time. But she supposed they had to stay in character in case anyone saw them—people were still leaving the bar—so she snuggled against him. "Find out anything useful tonight?"

He shrugged. "Nothing spectacular. Got a couple of names to run through the system. If there's a tunnel, you definitely win."

Good. She liked winning. She liked the idea of him coming to see her at last as an independent, competent woman, as opposed to Miss Disaster, a total screwup.

They walked and, even as they carefully scanned the few people lurching to their cars, they pretended to be looking at each other. Not really a hardship for her. He was totally hot. He always had been.

She couldn't see any movement at the car shop now as she gave the place a quick glance. The black pickup was gone. Brandon had probably driven off with whatever he'd been carrying in that box. Considering it was past 2:00 a.m., he might not come back tonight.

That would serve their purposes just fine, she thought. It'd be easier to snoop if nobody was around.

They walked past the car shop then entered the small convenience store. Shep headed to the back. "How about some iced tea?"

But while they were picking through the cooler, Brian walked in.

He nodded at them as he went for smokes, then ended up behind them at the checkout line. He managed a leering look at her legs. "Hey."

Shep nodded at him and added a handful of condoms to their purchases from the display before wrapping his arm around her waist. "Hey yourself."

Not too subtle, was he?

She thought about jabbing him in the ribs with her elbow as he paid then stuffed the foil packets into his back pocket, but all she could do was smile as she did her best to act her cover. She pulled him over by the magazine rack on their way out, pretending to be picking through the tabloids, so Brian would leave first. She wanted the manager gone so they could take a better look at the mechanic shop on their way back, unobserved.

His car was parked in front of the store. He got in and drove away.

They walked outside into the balmy night at last, and she looked after the car as it disappeared around the corner.

"Was that necessary?" She hissed the words under her breath. That many condoms? Really?

He flashed her an overly innocent look.

Fine. Whatever. She pushed back the aggravation and focused on the job. "I want to walk down the side street so we can check out the repair shop from the side and back. I want to get a better feel for it." A better feel for how to get in.

He looped his arm around her shoulders, keeping her close to him as they'd started out.

She would have preferred some space—her brain worked better that way—but to shake off his embrace would have meant admitting that he was affecting her. Instead, she draped her arm around his waist. Two could play this game.

The side street was badly lit and completely deserted. They kept an eye on the houses across the road while checking out the car shop from this angle. The shop didn't have a single light on in the back, either; it was completely dark. They cut through the parking lot, as if taking a shortcut to the Laundromat behind the mechanic's.

The shop's back door looked like a simple deal, with a simple lock, she saw when they got close enough. She stopped and turned into Shep, as if for a kiss, lifting her face to his. "I have a set of lock picks on me," she said as her body tingled from the contact.

"I'd feel more comfortable if I took you back to your hotel and came back here on my own."

Did he even realize that he was insulting her? "I'm an FBI agent."

His lips flattened for a second. "I know."

"I don't need your permission to do my job. And I certainly don't need your protection, although I'd be stupid not to accept backup. I'm going in."

He held her gaze, a pained look on his face. "When did you become so pushy?"

"I don't know what you're talking about."

A lone cowboy meandered down the side street. They had to wait until he passed out of sight. They kept their hands on each other, playing the part of lovers who'd stopped for a quick kiss and some sweet words.

Shep bent his head a little closer as they gazed at each other. "Why didn't you stay with music?" he asked out of the blue. "You sure know how to rock a stage."

Where had that come from? "Are you hoping I'll give up the FBI and go on tour?" A smile tugged at her lips. "You want me gone that bad?"

"You have no idea," he said with feeling.

A quick laugh escaped her. "I like the FBI. Not that I want to do it forever."

"What else?"

"I'd like to work with foster youth someday. I have some ideas about how to help kids who might be going down the wrong path." She gave a small shrug. "I have some experience there."

His face turned somber as he watched her. "Seventeen and all alone in the world. You shouldn't have run away."

"Stop saying that. I wouldn't be who I am if I hadn't." She tilted her head. "I'm good at what I do, too. You don't have to worry about me."

But he still hesitated another long minute before he said, "Okay. Let's see if there's an easy way into this place."

The cowboy had long disappeared down the street.

She moved away from Shep. "You carrying?"

He nodded.

He probably had a small weapon in his boot, since she couldn't see any bulges in his waistband behind his back.

"Me, too." She'd gotten a dainty little thing for her purse, something any woman would carry. She'd left her government-issue weapon in her hotel room. She kept her bag behind the bar while she sang, where anyone could have gone through it. If anyone snooped, she didn't want them to see anything that might give her away.

The back door was locked, but she made quick work of it.

He raised a dark eyebrow as they stepped inside. "You have a knack for this."

"A skill I had before I ever entered law enforcement, to be fair," she whispered back to him as they moved forward.

Three cars sat in the six-bay garage, no people in sight.

They moved along the wall, looking for a door that might lead down to the basement. Shep was the one to find it. Somebody had taped a piece of paper on the door that said W.C. OUT OF ORDER.

She worked the lock, again, nothing fancy. A super-security lock would have stood out, she supposed. She had it open within a minute. Instead of a bathroom, a staircase stretched down in front of them, dark and not very inviting.

He turned on the small LED light that hung from his keychain and went down first, past the rat droppings, then the mummified rat on the landing. She turned on her own keychain light and followed, closing and locking the door behind her in case they came out somewhere else. She didn't want anyone to know that somebody had been through here.

The stairs led straight down into a narrow passageway. They followed it and found nothing down there but bare brick walls, no room for anything, really.

There were a couple of turns, two branches that led off to empty storage rooms. They followed the main tunnel.

"Probably built during Prohibition," Shep said as they moved forward.

That would explain why it led to a bar.

Less than ten minutes passed before they

reached another set of stairs, the tunnel still continuing beyond.

They went up, through the door at top, careful not to make any noise. The lights were off, but enough moonlight came through the windows to illuminate the place. They were in a waiting room with old plastic chairs and a scuffed reception desk.

Scribbled-over posters about the food pyramid decorated the walls. To their left a supply closet stood with its door half-open, the shelves stocked with bottles of disinfectant and boxes of bandages. They had reached some kind of a health clinic it seemed.

They hadn't passed by one when they'd walked. Which meant the place had a different storefront. It was likely an illegal clinic, the cash-only type that asked for no ID and treated gunshot wounds without questions.

"Handy for the steroid pills," Shep whispered, moving forward.

Right. He'd gotten some of those from Tank. Sounded as if Brian and his crew had a hand in a number of things. They apparently appreciated the efficiency of diversifying.

"Nature abhors a vacuum, and so do criminal organizations," she said, keeping her voice down. "Do you think Brian is stepping into the gap that was created when your team took out some of the local big dogs?"

She would have said more, but as she stepped after him, voices reached them.

They weren't alone in the building.

Chapter Seven

Shep froze and held up a hand to alert Lilly, but from the look in her eyes, she'd heard the voices, too. There were at least two people in one of the back offices.

"How long are we supposed to sit around doing nothing?" a man asked in a deep, raspy voice. "I'm losing money every damn day."

"Lie low is the word," someone else answered. "You just cool your heels until the first."

October first, Shep thought. They already knew that the Coyote had put everything on hold until then, probably to lull CBP into thinking smuggling was slowing. Then on the first, when all his minions started up business again, the sheer volume would overwhelm the border agents. In the chaos, the Coyote could slip his special cargo through without being detected.

Not if Shep and his team had anything to do with it.

"I have creditors to pay," the man with the deeper voice said.

Lilly pulled away from Shep silently and pointed toward the half-open door of the supply closet. He nodded and moved after her, careful not to make any noise. They'd be out of sight in there in case anyone came out of that office, but they could still hear the conversation.

"Tell them to wait," the other man answered.

The closet was pretty tight, shelves taking up most of the space. While Lilly was looking, trying to figure out how they could both fit, he simply pressed himself into the far corner, where he wouldn't be seen even if they left the closet door half-open. They had to do that, leave everything the same so if the men came out, they wouldn't notice anything out of place.

Lilly shot him a dubious look, then wedged herself into the remaining space, her back pressed tightly against him, the only way they'd both remain concealed.

Her soft scent in his nose was bad enough. He could have handled that, but other things... Her bottom was crushed against him, firm and round and everything he shouldn't be thinking about.

Don't move, he said in silent prayer, trying his best to focus on the men who were still talking.

"I need one shipment tonight," the deeper of

the two voices was saying. "I have nothing. If I don't provide the merchandise, my buyers will go to someone else and I lose them."

"Put them off for a few days. Jonesing ain't never killed nobody."

"I've been playing that game for weeks. I need to give them something. I'm going over tonight."

"The hell you are." A chair scraped the floor, as though it were being shoved back.

"You gonna stop me?"

"If I have to."

The sounds of a scuffle filtered from the back office, then suddenly a gunshot rent the night. Then came the sound of a body hitting the floor with a dull thud.

Shep gripped his gun. He could feel Lilly tense, going for her own weapon.

"Are we gonna get in trouble for this with the boss?" a new, younger voice asked inside the office.

"You just keep your mouth shut," the deep-voiced man answered. "Dumb bastard thought he was gonna tell me what to do. Hell with that."

"What are we gonna do with him?"

"Leave him. We got a long night ahead of us. Ricky's on duty tonight at the border crossing. He won't give us no trouble."

Footsteps sounded, coming their way, boots

scuffing on the tile floor. Shep held his gun ready in his right hand, grabbed Lilly's hip with the left and pulled her even closer as he flattened himself tightly against the wall so they wouldn't be discovered.

He couldn't see anything from where he was. Maybe Lilly would catch a glimpse of the men. They each held their breath as the two walked by the supply closet.

The men didn't go to the door that led down to the secret tunnel. They went to the clinic's back exit that opened to the alley.

As soon as the door closed behind the men, Lilly and Shep hurried to the back door, but they didn't open it until they heard a car start, and even then just enough to catch a glimpse of a black Chevy Blazer and its license plate.

Shep pulled out his phone and called it in. Since his pickup was at The Yellow Armadillo, a full block away, there was no way they could catch up to these two.

He turned back to Lilly, holding the line. "Did you see them?"

"The younger one was Brandon from the bar," she said as she hurried away from him, back toward the room where the men had been arguing. "The other one I haven't seen before."

Shep passed that information on to the office.

"They're heading for the border-crossing station. They have a buddy there called Ricky."

"We'll follow them across, see who they make contact with," Ryder said at the other end. "You go back to your place and take your break. You have a shift in the morning. Those of us who are on duty will handle this." Ryder paused. "We're getting close to something. When this goes down, I want everyone in top shape. Keith's trip to San Antonio panned out. We know the target is one or more government buildings in Washington, D.C."

"That's a big step forward."

"And we'll take more until we get to the end of this. Now you go and take your break," Ryder said before the line went dead.

Shep followed Lilly into the office where the men had been talking. She was taking pictures of a dead guy with her phone.

He filled her in on the news from Ryder before asking "Do we know who he is?" as he gestured at the body with his head.

"Jack Alexander. Local guy, according to the address on his driver's license." She put her phone away. "Do we call in the cops?"

"That would be the correct procedure," he agreed.

"But we won't?"

"You're learning." He felt a smile tugging at

the corners of his lips. "Let the staff find him in the morning. We don't want to call attention to the fact that we were here. Any objections?"

"I'm not here to make your job more difficult. I'm here to help."

He hesitated a few seconds as he watched the earnest expression on her face. "All right."

She nodded and gave him a smile, a sincere one, not like the ones she flashed around at the bar. "Thanks for treating me like a real partner. I appreciate it."

She looked genuinely pleased, as if he'd given her a gift. Her eyes were all lit up and shining at him. Some unnamed emotion stirred inside his chest.

"Let's go," he said and turned from her, going back to the basement.

She padded after him, making sure she locked the door behind them.

They followed the tunnel to a sudden stop where iron bars with a massive lock barred their way. Lilly's picks failed here miserably. One bent nearly in half.

"We need more to get through here." She stood after twenty minutes of hard trying.

"TNT?" he suggested.

"My kind of guy." She laughed, but then she shook her head. "Come on, cowboy, we're not going to reach the bar through here tonight." She walked back in the direction they'd come from, keeping her LED light in front of her.

He had a hard time directing the light from his. It kept illuminating her long legs in the short skirt she'd worn onstage. He refused to look at the winding flowers of her tattoo as it disappeared under the fabric.

She was talking about the tools she needed and wondering aloud if she could get them tonight so they could come back before the stores opened in the morning. Probably not, she concluded and sounded damned disappointed.

And he realized miserably that he liked this new Lilly Tanner. She was exactly the kind of woman that a man like him could fall in love with.

He couldn't afford to let his guard down for a minute.

To Lilly's relief, they got back to his pickup without trouble and without running into anyone they knew from the bar.

Shep remained silent. Almost brooding, which was kind of strange, since he wasn't the brooding type. He was the type to take action if something bothered him.

They stopped by the pickup and he looked at her, his gaze searching her face. Was he still upset that she was here, that she'd been inserted into the middle of his op?

"I can just walk back to the hotel," she offered. If he needed space, she could certainly give him some—at least tonight—even if she couldn't withdraw from the op. And a brisk walk might help as she processed the latest developments.

"The hotel is on my way." And then he reached out, took her arm and backed her against the truck in one smooth move, and kissed her.

And it was *not* one of those lips-brushing-against-lips almost-kisses he'd planted on her before for show. This time he kissed her as if he meant it. With the adrenaline of tonight's work still coursing through her, she responded, her arms going around his neck as his hands grabbed for her hips.

Instant heat. Or maybe not so "instant," considering. The moment had years' worth of teenage fantasies behind it. If the sudden, overwhelming need was more than just a blast from the past, she didn't want to think about it.

His right hand slid up to her breast and cupped it. *Zing.* She moaned in pleasure and he used the advantage. His tongue swept in to kiss her deeper.

Oh.

All her senses were buzzing, her body screaming that she wanted this. And maybe she somehow telepathically communicated that, because the next thing she knew he was opening the pickup's door and she was sideways on the passenger seat as he stood in front of her, her legs wrapped around his waist.

Her hands slid up his side, to his back. He had a great body, the kind that made a woman want to run her fingers all over it. Since he didn't look as if he would protest, she did. The thin shirt he wore didn't provide much impediment. She could feel every muscle, every hill and valley.

He was hard everywhere, and he ground that hardness against her, against the aching need where her thighs met. Heat rushed to that spot. Another moan escaped her throat.

Which was beyond strange because she normally wasn't the zero-to-sixty-in-three-seconds kind of girl.

But his hand on her breast was doing amazing things, his clever fingers teasing her nipple into a hard knob. She ached for him there, too. She ached for him everywhere.

In the middle of a stupid parking lot, on the front seat of a pickup. So not her. She might have been acting the tough rock chick onstage, but in the bedroom…she was more the type to turn out the light when it came to intimacy.

And none of this was real, in any case. They'd

been pretending to be a couple all night, touching and kissing. Neither of them had significant others. Both could have used some release. But she couldn't be casual with Shep. The last thing she wanted was to start falling for him again.

She didn't trust anyone with her heart, and especially not Shep Lewis, who'd already rejected her once.

"This is crazy," she mumbled against his lips. "We have to stop." Before it was too late.

He immediately pulled away and stared at her, breathing hard.

She tried to gather some shreds of sanity about her. "We should…" Should what? She couldn't finish it, because what her body and her mind wanted were two different things.

And after a long moment, he stepped away.

The shock of separation had her body protesting. She pressed her lips together so she wouldn't beg him to come back to her. She pulled her legs into the car.

His expression darkened as he watched her, his eyes narrowing with suspicion as if he was thinking maybe she'd somehow tricked him into the kiss.

"I—" She closed her mouth, not sure, again, how to proceed.

He walked around to the other side, got into the car and slammed the door behind him. "I shouldn't have. I'm sorry. It's not going to happen again, dammit."

That should have made her feel reassured. Instead, it made her feel disappointed. They drove to the hotel in the most awkward silence she could imagine.

Instead of dropping her off at the front door, he pulled into the parking lot.

"I'm coming up," he told her as he shut off the engine.

Judging by the dark clouds that sat on his face, his visit wouldn't be to finish what they'd started.

She got out, more than ready to leave him and have some time to herself to recover. "We don't have to hash this out tonight." Or ever.

"We do. And I—" He hesitated, then pulled a folder from the backseat and came after her. "I meant to show you something."

Did his team find information he hadn't had a chance to share with her yet?

They went up in the elevator. This time it was just the two of them, nobody out this late, but he didn't say a word to her until they got up to her floor and they were inside her suite.

"Things can't go on like this," he said at last, standing inside the door. "You shouldn't be here. It's dangerous, and it's—"

"I can handle it."

"Well, maybe I can't," he snapped, holding her gaze. "I don't know what to do with this."

By *this* he meant the attraction between them, she guessed.

"We'll ignore it." She wasn't even sure if it was real. Did she really want him, *this* Shep, or was it something left over from the past?

"Because that's worked so well until now." A wry smile tilted up his lips. "The bar is a dangerous place. Brian is up to his neck in smuggling."

"It's just one last night. If we find a clue, it'd be worth anything. And you don't have to worry about me. I'm an FBI agent," she reminded him.

He shook his head. "I don't seem to be able to catch up to that."

Was that it? He came up to talk her into quitting and going home?

Anger lit a small flame inside her. He didn't think she was good enough. For the job. Or for him. She stiffened her spine. Nobody ever thought she was good enough. Not her parents, who'd sold her for drugs, not the couple who bought her then threw her away, not the system she'd ended up in.

She stepped back. "You should go. It's late."

"Are you walking away from the bar?"

"I'll do the job I came here to do, and I'll thank you for not interfering."

"Lilly—"

"Do you ever try to talk your teammates into taking it easy on their job and walking away from danger?"

His forehead drew into an annoyed frown. "No," he admitted.

"I assume you work with outside law enforcement from time to time. How about them?"

He watched her for a few long seconds. "Fine. I get your point."

"I'm not the same person I was ten years ago."

"No kidding," he said miserably.

It nearly made her smile, squashing her anger. "What bothers you more, the fact that the FBI sent someone to keep an eye on you guys, or that you're attracted to me?"

He shot her a dark look. "They're both wrong. Neither should be happening."

"Tough cookies." He used to tell her that all the time back in the day.

"The team will get the job done. You shouldn't be here." He paused. "You shouldn't look like this," he said accusingly. "And I shouldn't have kissed you. Not for show, and most definitely not for real."

She bit back a smile.

"Quit looking so damn pleased."

She let the smile bloom. "You don't get disconcerted every day. You'll just have to forgive me if I take a moment to enjoy it."

She took her time. Then shook her head. "Listen, seven years of age difference when I was seventeen and you were twenty-four might have seemed like a lot. It's not now. I'm not in your charge or under your protection."

"You're under my protection," he said unequivocally and stood there all wide shouldered and tough looking.

He'd tried to protect her back in the day. She couldn't let him. Too many people had let her down by that point. So she'd left Shep before he could let her down, too. She'd run away.

She glanced at the folder in his hand. "What did you want to show me?"

He followed her gaze, his eyebrows furrowing as if he'd forgotten about his papers. He hesitated for a moment before holding the folder out for her. "Your case file from ten years ago. After you disappeared, I emailed the files to myself so I could work on them at home. I did my best to find you." He cleared his throat. "I realized the other day that I might still have them in that old email account. I did."

Her mouth went dry as she took the folder.

She drew a deep breath before opening it, took a look at the document on top, then paged carefully through the others. She scanned the list of foster homes, medical checkups, a list of her bad behaviors, grade cards, a report on the circumstances of how she'd come into foster care—found abandoned at a bus stop.

But what really got to her were the pictures. Her smiling at six or seven. Her looking sullen a few years later, holding a scruffy cat. Her throat tightened. She'd forgotten about the cat.

She closed the file and put it on the desk, needing a moment, then looked up into his dark eyes.

He'd given her back her missing years. Something to fill some of the empty spaces in her life. As if he'd somehow seen into her heart and knew exactly what was missing.

Maybe she could trust him just a little. She swallowed. "I appreciate it. Thanks."

He nodded and turned to leave.

"Wait." She stepped closer. She didn't want him to leave yet, but she wasn't sure what to say. "We have a complicated relationship."

He nodded, watching her face.

"I wasn't sure how it would be. I mean, us meeting again." The people you cared for, the ones who were supposed to protect you, always let you down. Or sold you for coke. "I don't do relationships." But she did want him in the here and now, this edgier Shep who sometimes looked at her as if he could devour her.

His masculine lips twisted into a wry smile. "Me, neither. I want you." He echoed her thoughts. "Pretty much all the time now. It's driving me crazy."

She took another step closer to him.

He held her gaze. "Lilly?"

She watched him and waited.

"Say no," he said as he reached out and pulled her into his strong arms.

She said nothing.

He lowered his head, fitted his lips to hers. "Tell me to get the hell out of here," he murmured.

It would have been the smart thing to do, probably. But her lips were tingling. So she pressed them a little closer to his.

He capitulated with a groan and wrapped his arms fully around her, gathered her tightly to his chest and tasted her.

Her knees turned weak. It didn't matter. He was holding her up. All those muscles came in handy at a time like this.

He licked the seam of her lips then nibbled on the bottom lip again, scraped his teeth against it. And when she opened up for him at last, he didn't hesitate. He took all that she offered. He took thoroughly.

Since her boots had heels, he was just a few inches taller than her and they fit together perfectly. He was all hard male and she was…a puddle of need, frankly.

He eased his hands down her sides, splayed his fingers over her hips as he held her to him. The tube top left her midriff bare and he took advantage, his thumbs moving in a circular motion on her skin, sending delicious shivers across her abdomen and lower.

His hands soon moved up an inch, then another. They pushed up the lacy material in front of them as they went, baring more and more of her to his seeking fingers. His touch was so featherlight and gentle, it melted the last of her resistance. The twin assault of his tongue and those clever fingers was almost more than she could handle.

She grabbed on to his waist for support. And then somehow his shirt came untucked, and her fingers sneaked under the material, coming into contact with his warm skin. There was nothing soft about the man, she thought as her fingers wandered upward over the muscles of his abdomen, up to his wide chest and tangled in a smattering of hair, her palms covering his impressive pecs.

He shifted them slowly, her back against the door, then took his hands off her, bracing them on either side of her head as he pulled back a few inches. "Tell me to leave."

If she were half as smart as she'd thought she was, she would have. Instead, she said, "Stay."

Her tube top was history the next second, his lips back on hers as his hands cupped her breasts through the flimsy silk of her strapless bra. He trailed kisses to her ear, bit then sucked the lobe.

Then she couldn't think anymore, because one of his clever hands slipped behind her and unclasped the bra. The other tugged the silk at the front and her breasts spilled free.

He pulled his head back from her cheek and kissed a trail of heat along her jaw, then down her neck, then circled her breasts before heading to one nipple first then the other.

His mouth was moist and hot on her, and she could feel more moisture and heat gather between her legs. All her life, she kept people at arm's length, yet now she couldn't get close enough to him. Nothing would be close enough until he was inside her.

Because that was where they were heading, she realized. They weren't at the bar or in the parking lot. Nothing to stop them here from taking this all the way.

The thought scared her and excited her in equal measure.

As if reading her mind, he hooked his hands under her bottom and lifted her off her feet. When she wrapped her legs around his waist, they were lined up perfectly, if not for some inconvenient denim.

She could have sent him away and pretended, for the sake of their jobs, that she didn't want him, but it would have been a lie. He was a decadelong itch under her skin. He was her first sexual fantasy, and he was a damned good one at that. So she was going to go with the impulses that told her to rip off his shirt.

When she did, he flashed her a dark grin and carried her to the bed to lay her down on top of the covers. "Are you sure?"

"Yes." She reached for him.

"Why?" he wanted to know.

The emotions that suddenly bubbled up in her chest she couldn't admit even to herself, let alone to him. So instead, she said, "Better get it out of our system. Then we can work together without the distraction, without wondering."

Sounded better than the pathetic *Because I've been in love with you since I was seventeen*. In any case, that wasn't true. Was it?

He tossed his shirt on the floor then kicked off his boots and lay down next to her. Since she was naked to the waist, he began working on her tight denim skirt.

She reached for his rodeo belt buckle, nervous suddenly and wondering if it was even possible that this could measure up to her insanely high expectations.

"Nothing is ever as good as we anticipate it," she said out loud without meaning to.

And when he threw her a questioning look, she added in way of explanation, "It'll be better once we go for it then accept the disappointment. Then we can concentrate on the tunnel and the smuggling."

He looked at her as if she was crazy.

The belt gave at last and she tugged down his zipper. His erection sprung free, barely held by his briefs. He was *very* happy to see her, from the looks of it.

He yanked off her skirt then hooked a finger under her lacy G-string. "What the hell is this? You can't afford proper underwear?" His voice sounded a shade weaker than before.

"I get hot dancing around the stage." The less clothes the better.

"Hot," he repeated, looking dazed, his eyes fixed on those few square inches of lace. Then he gave a quick grin. "Everybody gets hot when you dance around the stage."

With that one hooked finger he drew the material down her legs then let it drop.

She lay naked before him.

He came to his feet next to the bed just long enough to shrug out of his jeans and underwear, never removing his gaze from her body. As he shook his jeans out, a handful of foil packets scattered on the bed by her feet.

"So we give in this once then forget about it?" he asked.

"Just to get it out of the way. Get the distraction over and done with," she told him. "We—"

But he bent suddenly and lay his index finger over her lips. And then, as he lay down next to her, he replaced the finger with his mouth, his finger slowly moving lower, skating across her skin to her knee, down her winding tattoo, caressing every flower and leaf then back up again to the V of her thighs. And then his long fingers parted her.

Pleasure flashed through her as he found the spot that was throbbing for him, aching with need. His mouth worked on hers while his finger worked down below. And when she was on the brink, he moved over on top and slid into her.

He didn't take it slow. He didn't move inch by tantalizing inch. He pushed forward as if he meant it and thrust into her all the way, making her moan his name as pleasure suffused her and dizzied her brain.

He filled her, stretched her, made her bones melt as he thrust in and out and picked up the rhythm. Her knees hooked around his narrow hips and she gave her body up to him completely.

He didn't take his time with this step, either. He lifted her higher and higher with ruthless efficiency, barely allowing her to catch her breath. Then her body contracted around him and she felt like a fireworks rocket, bursting into a shower of sparkles, flying.

SHEP LAY NEXT to her, spent and stunned, staring at the ceiling. A part of his world had shattered and he didn't know how to piece it back together, didn't know how to process what had just happened between them.

It had seemed so right, so easy. Yet now, as sanity returned, he had to seriously reevaluate his actions. He had to take responsibility for the way he'd lost control.

"I didn't come up with this in mind, I swear."

She made some sleepy sounds. "I'm not complaining."

Yet the fact remained that he *had* come up to her hotel room and made love to her. She'd been tired after work and…confused. He'd taken advantage of her. That was the way Jamie would see it. And Mitch. He winced.

He had no idea how to make this right.

"Marry me," he blurted as he looked at her and tried hard not to want her again, tried and failed. His body was stirring already. Insanity.

She turned to him, wide-eyed and a lot more

awake now, as a succession of emotions crossed her face. "What?"

"Jamie and Mitch are going to kill me for this."

Her eyes narrowed. "Did you just ask me to marry you because of Jamie and Mitch?"

He looked at her miserably.

She sat up in the bed. "Get out." She bit out the words. "I want you to leave."

He sat up, too. "I should have protected you. Even from myself—"

She growled as she punched him.

Chapter Eight

Shep stood in Ryder's office and watched the interrogation through the two-way mirror, rubbing his jaw where Lilly had socked him the night before. He'd deserved it. He still felt guilty as hell for going up to her room. Shouldn't have done it. Should have never made love to her.

Last night had been an epic fail as far as getting her out of his system went. He wanted her now more than ever.

Jamie shifted next to him, his attention on the men in the other room. "The National Guard arrived at Fort Sam Houston. Supposedly for a joint exercise."

But in reality, so they'd be close enough to swoop in at the last minute if his team failed, Shep thought. He should have been thinking about that and the interrogation in the other room, but his thoughts kept skipping back to Lilly.

Jamie looked at him. "You're quiet today."

"Didn't get enough sleep last night."

Jamie raised an eyebrow.

Shep pretended to be engrossed in Mo and Ryder handling the questioning. Brandon, handcuffed to the chair, was trying to make a deal, giving testimony against his buddy.

Mo stood over him, looking damn impressive when he did his looming thing. "I don't care who did the shooting last night. We need the big boss down south. The Coyote. Who is he?"

"I don't know who he is, man. He's at the top of the totem pole. He's got powerful friends. When he don't like somebody, they're dead." The guy hunched his back. "If he even thinks I'm talking, I'll be ground to pulp, man."

Ryder and Keith had followed Brandon and his friend over to Mexico, watched the transaction. Keith had stayed to follow their Mexican link and see where that led. Ryder followed them back and had them apprehended at the border, along with their border-agent friend.

After Mo was done with the interrogation, he escorted Brandon out into the deputy sheriff's custody, and they switched to the border agent, Ricky Lowell.

"You know what happens to former law-enforcement officers in federal prison?" Mo started, not pulling any punches.

"Nothing worse than a shot in the head, which

is what I'll get in some dark alley if I tell you anything." The man leaned back in his chair, all cool and playing the tough guy, the opposite of what Brandon had been.

"I heard that. The Coyote doesn't mess around. He can reach anyone anywhere."

Ricky shrugged. "I'm not going to give him a reason to want to reach me. You're wasting your time here."

Mo played things just as cool. "We put the word out that you talked. When he sends an assassin, we'll catch that guy and follow him back to the Coyote. I don't care how we catch the bastard, as long as we catch him. I doubt the death of a corrupt border agent will weigh too heavily on my conscience."

Ricky shifted in his seat. "You can't do that."

"Wanna bet?"

"You're not going to catch whoever he sends. He's got men everywhere."

"A chance I'm willing to take," Mo promised. "It'll either work or not. You're not talking, so half a chance is better than no chance."

Ricky swore. "I want a lawyer. Where the hell am I, anyway? I want to be transported out of here. You're consultants for the CBP. You don't even have jurisdiction over me."

"You'd be surprised at the kind of leeway I

have." Mo shifted closer. "We need the Coyote. We need him yesterday."

"I have rights."

"Rights are flexible in cases like this. We're talking about border security. You compromise it on a daily basis from what we hear. What if some terrorists were to sneak through?"

"But they didn't—" Ricky went white, all the coolness sliding right off his face as he understood at last. He swallowed. "You can't link me to terrorism. It's not true. You can't make that up. What the hell? I want an attorney. I want to know what I'm being charged with."

"You know damn well terror suspects get none of that." Mo waited, letting the silence grow heavy. "Maybe you understand your situation better now. Why don't you take a moment to weigh your options?"

Ricky didn't need long, less than ten seconds, before he blurted out, "I don't know who he is, all right? Nobody knows. He's some bigwig over in Mexico."

"A crime boss?"

"That, but more."

Mo paused. "Politician?"

"Maybe. I don't know. All I know is he has money and power to make things happen. He leads a double life. That's why nobody can know who he really is or what his real name is."

"Who else works for him at CBP?"

His gaze shifted. "I don't know."

"The more useful you are, the better things will go for you," Mo reminded him.

"I don't know all of them," Ricky said. "I know a couple." And then, reluctantly, he named three men.

Out in the other room, Jamie moved toward the door. "I'll go pick them up."

"I'll go with you," Shep offered.

"I'll be fine. You stay and handle whatever else actionable intel Mo gets out of the bastard."

Ricky was begging on the other side of the two-way mirror as Jamie left. "You have to keep me safe."

Mo didn't look concerned. "You'll be safe in prison. You keep talking and I'll arrange for solitary confinement."

"Up north." His eyes hung on Mo. "The Coyote has men down south everywhere."

"How about Ohio?"

The man nodded.

And Mo said, "But you'll have to earn it."

Sweat beaded on Ricky's forehead. "I know a couple of mules. The regulars that always come through during my shift. They've been taking a break lately, but they'll be back soon. You can catch them in action."

"All right, we'll start with that."

Shep wrote down the names. He was about to leave to pick them up when Ricky volunteered another bit of information.

"All smuggling is on hold until the first."

"Why is that?" Mo asked. They had their suspicions, but confirmation would have been helpful, knowing that they were on the right path.

"Don't know that." Ricky's expression switched to sly. "But there was a…request. On the first, I'm not to assign Galmer's Gulley to anyone for patrol. Like an oversight thing. You might catch someone there."

"Only at Galmer's Gulley?"

"Solitary up north?"

Mo nodded.

Rickey hesitated, but then spit it out at last. "And I'm supposed to thin the patrol schedule that day as much as I can. Approve more vacation days than usual. But put nobody at Galmer's Gulley."

Galmer's Gulley, Shep thought as he headed out to pick up the six smugglers on his list. He was smiling. They very likely had the time and place for the terrorists' transfer. Exactly the breakthrough they needed.

Confirmation would have been nice, though. And he might very well get that from one of the smugglers he was about to grab. He ran their names through the police database, printed the rap sheets, which included current employment and home addresses.

He ran into Lilly in the parking lot.

"Hey." She was just coming in, dressed like a local in blue jeans, boots, a T-shirt with a lone star over her chest and a cowboy hat shading her head. She'd assimilated pretty darn fast. She shot him a dark look.

He had no idea what to say to her. What did a man say after a night like the one they'd just spent together? He wanted more but, of course, he couldn't very well tell her that.

She didn't wait for him to figure out a game plan. Her fine lips pressed together. "Any progress with the op?" She was all cool and professional, as if last night hadn't happened.

If she could act that way, so could he. He channeled his thoughts away from the tangled sheets. "We got the crossing point. I'm heading out to pick up some smugglers to see if they have any further details or confirmation."

Relief settled on her face. "Okay. That's good." She walked straight to his SUV instead of the stairs. "I'm going with you."

The word *no* was on his tongue. But he didn't want her to think that he couldn't handle what had happened between them the night before. So, instead, he said, "Be my guest."

And it was the last thing he said to her until

they reached the first address, a chicken processing plant. Two men on his list, brothers, worked there.

He picked them up without trouble and dropped them off for holding at the Pebble Creek sheriff's office, leaving them in Bree's capable hands until they could be interrogated. He called Mo to let him know he'd have another batch waiting as soon as he was done with the border agent.

The next man on the list didn't have a permanent address, but did have half a dozen locations where he was known to hang out. The Yellow Armadillo was one of them.

"Know him?" Shep showed the printed mug shot to Lilly.

"I might have seen him at the bar." She thought for a second. "I'm pretty sure I have. He came in after hours, the first time I was there to see Brian."

"We'll catch him at the bar later today, then." Shep moved on to the next name.

This one lived in Pebble Creek. Nothing listed for employer. He drove to the address listed, a small ranch home on the outskirts of town.

"Why are you looking for Joey?" his mother wanted to know after she'd opened the door to their knock.

"We'd like to ask for his assistance in a police matter. Is he home, ma'am?"

"He's with his friends. They volunteer cleaning up around the high school. They're good kids."

Shep drove off to look for him.

Having Lilly within reach, the light scent of her perfume lingering in the cab, a truckload of unsaid things between them, was messing with his head. He tried to push all that aside and just focus on the job.

Joey's cleaning up the road by the high school turned out to be selling weed by the high school. He took off running when he spotted Shep heading for him.

But Lilly had already gone around, stepped out from behind a pickup in the parking lot and decked the man.

"Joey Manito, you're under arrest for possession and distribution." Shep cuffed him, pulled him up and walked him to his SUV as he read him his rights.

Since there was still room in the back, he didn't take Joey to jail just yet. He drove off to the next address.

The small house, just a step up from a shack, stood deserted.

"Any other info?" Lilly asked, picking up the

guy's rap sheet. She scanned the paper. There was no employment listed.

"Car?"

She nodded.

"We can call the Pebble Creek deputy sheriff and have an APB put out on the license plate," he suggested, and that was exactly what Lilly did while he drove to the next address they had.

They didn't run into any problems there. The man was so stoned he couldn't have run if he tried. He sang raunchy Mexican folk songs all the way to the Pebble Creek jail.

Shep stepped into the deputy's office while Lilly dealt with the paperwork.

"Anything on the APB?"

"I'll let you know the second I have something. Everything okay?"

"The usual nonsense." He considered Bree for a second. "If a bigwig was running all the smuggling from the other side of the border, who would be your best guess?"

She leaned back in her chair as she tapped her index finger on the desk.

"Politician? Chief of police?" he suggested.

"I don't think so. They're on the take, but not running things. What I know of the ones I'm thinking of…can't see them as a criminal mastermind. Mostly they're men who got put into positions by their wealthy fathers. They know how to take money, not make it. Top criminals are rarely politicians—too much media scrutiny. They buy politicians for their needs."

Lilly came looking for him. "Ready?"

"I'll let you know if I think of anything," Bree promised him before they left.

"She's very beautiful," Lilly remarked on their way to his car.

"She used to be Miss Texas."

"She was smiling at you." They got in.

"She's very smiley."

"Are you and her…" Lilly's face was a tight mask, without emotion.

He blinked. "Jealous?" For some reason the thought made him happy.

"Not in the least," she snapped. "She's welcome to have you."

He started the engine. "I don't think Jamie would agree with that."

She didn't say anything, but her shoulders noticeably relaxed.

Had she really been jealous? Did that mean last night hadn't been just a gigantic spur-of-the-moment mistake for her? He wasn't sure what it'd been for him. He was still evaluating it.

He didn't say that, however. In fact, they didn't talk about anything personal for the rest of the day. He'd apologized for making love to her. She hadn't liked it. He'd asked her to marry him. She hadn't liked that, either.

He wanted to figure out what she wanted from him so he could avoid her decking him again.

The sixth man on their list gave them the runaround. They'd go to one address, be told he had moved. Go to the next, be told he temporarily lived someplace else. And it kept up like that. The man had disappeared.

"Could be he's been killed," Shep said as he dropped Lilly off in front of her hotel at the end of the day. No way was he going up. Ever again.

"Or got tipped off that we're rounding up smugglers," she said as she turned from him.

He didn't stay to watch her walk away. He stepped on the gas and drove off before he could do something stupid.

Lilly stood by the window in her hotel room and looked out into the approaching darkness. Better than looking at the bed. Heat flooded her every time she did that.

Shep seemed determined to ignore their night together. Because he thought it was a mistake. Because he still thought of her as some young idiot under his authority. She could have screamed with frustration.

She'd sung her sets on Saturday night, and he'd shown up, supposedly to protect her, but that was all. Brian had been his slimy self, the crowd as drunk and rowdy as the night before. The band got it into their heads that they wanted to get to know her better, so she hadn't had a minute alone between sets, hadn't gotten a chance to investigate any further.

After her last set ended, Shep brought her home again, in silence, let her out in front of the hotel then drove away.

She refused to beg for his attention again. If he wanted to ignore what had happened between them, she wasn't going to bring it up if it killed her.

So she spent her Sunday with busywork, typing up a long report for her boss at the FBI and sending it off, then running personal errands all day. By the time night fell, she was tired from running around but her mind was too antsy to rest. When her phone rang, she grabbed for it, thinking it might be Shep....

She had no idea what to hope for.

She didn't want to fall in love with him.

But Jamie Cassidy's voice came through the line instead. "Hey, want to go grab something to eat? Unless you have other plans."

Right. Because her social life was so happening. Hardly. Yet, she still hesitated. She wasn't good at letting people in.

Then she drew a deep breath and plunged forward. "I'm game. But shouldn't you be on a hot date with the deputy sheriff?"

"Nothing's more important than family," he said, which made her feel good. "Anyway, it's girls' night out. Bree is taking her sister to the mall. They're getting pedicures and eyebrow shaping, whatever that means. I'd rather not know the sordid details. I have an hour before I go back on duty."

He didn't sound very threatening. And an hour seemed manageable. "Know any good pizza places?"

"Sure. But there's a chipotle *cocina* not far from the hotel that will make you glad you came to Texas. I'll pick you up."

"I'll meet you there." She always preferred to have her own ride. It was an independence thing. "Just let me know where it is."

He did. "How soon can you be ready?"

She laughed out loud. "I'm an FBI agent."

"Right. Born ready and all that."

"You bet." He was easy to talk to, she thought as she hung up.

She'd barely seen him since she'd arrived. The team was working full steam, everyone pursuing leads, the team members off gathering information and tracking down any possible connections to the Coyote. They were all running around nearly 24/7, with breaks that were few and far between.

She'd meant to catch up with Jamie, just hadn't found the right moment yet.

Family was new to her. But now that she had some, maybe she could explore the possibilities a little. Without going in too deep. She didn't fully trust the idea of one big happy family. Had never seen one truly work, up close and personal.

Her only experience was that the second she let her guard down and let people into her heart, they dumped her or hurt her. Her operating life rule had been not to trust. Part of her equated that with keeping herself safe. It was a false assumption and an unhelpful rule, however.

Past experiences created life assumptions that influenced one's attitude toward life and his or her actions, which formed their new life experiences. She'd spent enough time with the FBI shrink to know that. She had to, to pass a psych evaluation for the job.

Understanding her hang-ups, however, and shaking off old habits were two different things. But she knew what she wanted: to move forward. She wasn't about to let the past bind her forever.

So while she didn't feel a big wave of warmth and pleasure at the thought of building some kind of family link with Jamie, she made herself go. Just as she would make herself give him a chance.

She brushed her hair and changed her T-shirt. She walked down the stairs instead of taking the elevator, needing the exercise. The drive wasn't long. The *cocina* was just a few blocks from her hotel, run by a family who'd been in the area before there was Texas, according to a framed newspaper article near the front door. The place was loud but smelled amazing, and Jamie had somehow managed to find them a quiet corner where they could talk without having to shout at each other.

"Do you live around here?" she asked once she slid into the booth across the table from him.

"Renting a place in the unsavory section. The better to keep an eye on the local troublemakers." He grinned.

Their order was delivered in minutes. They were sharing a chipotle chicken-and-shrimp platter that just about covered the small table.

"I met your sister, Megan," she said, wanting to start with something positive. "She helped my brother find me. She's very nice."

"You think that because you didn't have to grow up with her," he said in a droll tone. "Once she put pink nail polish on me while I was sleeping. Sisters are the devil's instrument. Be glad you have a brother."

She couldn't help the laugh that escaped her. "When was that?" She popped a shrimp into her mouth. It tasted like heaven.

"Don't know. Tried to repress the memory as best I could. Middle school maybe."

"I'm sure you did your best to annoy her, too."

He studiously kept his gaze on the platter. "I'm not saying I never cut her hair. Or shoved the odd frog or lizard down her shirt." He flashed a nostalgic grin as he looked up.

"You have a ton of brothers. Seven?" She popped a giant shrimp into her mouth and let the flavor spread through her.

He sobered for a moment. "Six now. Billy was killed in action." He paused. "But when we were kids, the seven of them put together were less trouble than Megan."

"I missed that," she told him as an old sense of longing awakened inside her. "The family thing. I have no memories of my birth family." And although she'd met Mitch and spent an entire afternoon with him, it still felt a little strange.

"So I take it when Mitch showed up on your doorstep, you didn't recognize him?" He shook his head. "Of course you didn't. You were a toddler when you last saw him. That had to be strange." He took a sip of his drink. "Him showing up out of the blue."

"I thought he was some scam artist. He was lucky I didn't put him on his back."

Jamie choked on his drink for a second before he finally swallowed. "I would have paid money to see that." He coughed some more. "You ever go up against Shep by any chance? And if you did, is there video footage?" He grinned.

She took a big bite of chicken so she wouldn't have to answer.

Jamie narrowed his eyes. "His jaw looked kind of purplish this morning."

Yeah. She'd seen that. She kept chewing in silence.

"If he's getting fresh with you…if you want me to beat him up, just say the word. That's what family is for."

She rolled her eyes. "There's way too much testosterone in that office. What is it with men and violence?"

He had the gall to look hurt. "What are you talking about? You're the one who socked him."

"I shouldn't have." She really regretted that. She sighed. "I ruined his life, you know. Back then."

He didn't look too concerned. "You were

probably the most excitement he saw until he joined the team. It was good training."

"I was on the wild side," she admitted.

"I heard." He took a bite of his food before he asked, "So what's the first thing that you do remember?"

"Foster families. Lots of them. I got passed around. I might have acted out now and then." She took a drink as she remembered. "The adults were all right. The kids…" She shook her head. "In places it was so bad you didn't dare fall asleep. Cutting my hair off in my sleep would have been the least of it. You had to show you were the toughest. Then you got in trouble for that."

"Is that how you ended up with Shep as your parole officer?"

She nodded. "He was okay. Not that I appreciated that at the time. I just wanted to be free."

They talked some more about that, then Jamie's brothers, and Megan and her new baby.

"I'm an aunt." The thought still made her a little dazed.

Jamie watched her. "How do you feel about that?"

"Weirder than weird. I'm linked to this little kid. And I'm supposed to be someone she can look up to and depend on if needed, and all that. Scary."

"I know what you mean." He nodded. "As long as they don't ask us to change diapers, right?"

She swallowed. "That ever happens, I'm joining the navy. I'd feel more comfortable with shipping out, honestly."

Jamie looked as if he'd considered the same. But when he spoke again, it was to change the subject. "So, you and Shep?" He shook his head. "Just trying to wrap my mind around it. I feel like I should ask him about his intentions."

"Don't." She looked down at her food. "It's over. It never really was anything."

"Okay. Just want to let you know that if you need me for any reason, I'm here. I'm family. I got your back."

A different person might have taken that as a good thing, but it just brought all of Lilly's insecurities to the surface. Why the hell did everyone want to protect her? First Shep, and now Jamie. Didn't they think she was good enough to stand on her own? She was.

She gave Jamie a flat smile and changed the subject, back to the family and all those other brothers-in-law she hadn't yet met. And by the end, she might have relaxed a little, laughing at Jamie's outrageous stories.

They stayed for an hour, then parted ways in front of the *cocina,* Jamie promising to invite her over for dinner and introduce her to his girls. Apparently, Katie, Bree's sister, lived with her.

She thought about that on her drive back, how Jamie seemed happy. That hadn't always been the case, from what she understood from the one-page summary she'd gotten on him before taking the job. He'd lost both legs, dealt with some serious PTSD in the past and heavy-duty depression. He'd been assigned to the team strictly for office duty in the beginning.

Dinner with him had been nice, but she was still antsy. So instead of heading straight to the hotel, she took a small detour to drive by The Yellow Armadillo.

Just because the bar was closed on Sundays, it didn't mean there wouldn't be anybody there. In fact, their day off might be the perfect time for Brian to run his illegal activities.

She wanted to find something, wanted progress, wanted to prove to Shep and Jamie and the rest of the team that she was good enough, that she could take care of business. That she didn't need them, didn't need anyone. Her pride didn't like that they all saw her as someone who needed to be protected.

Of course, pride was a dangerous thing. Especially when it went hand in hand with her deep-seated need to always prove herself, always stand alone, never trust a hand offered.

Pride goes before the fall. Unfortunately, she didn't remember that bit of ageless wisdom until it was too late.

Chapter Nine

The sign on the door said CLOSED, but the lights were on behind the shuttered blinds. Maybe they'd been left on for security. Most of the stores on the street were lit up. Still, on an impulse, Lilly drove around the block.

A small truck idled in the back alley, blocking her view, the empty cab facing out, the back lined up with the bar as if for loading. All right, so that could be something interesting.

She thought about calling Jamie, but he was headed to work, and dragging him back on a hunch didn't seem fair. It'd be taking him away from following other leads that might actually pan out. First she'd see if there was anything to call about. She didn't want to seem like some overeager rookie jumping the gun, trying to make something out of nothing.

She looped back to the front and parked, then got out. The parking lot was deserted, less than a dozen cars, all of which probably belonged to the people who lived in the apartments above some of the shops. None of the businesses were open this time of the night on a Sunday, no reason for anyone else to be here.

She walked up to the bar and tried to look through the gap in the blinds. But before she could have gotten a good look, the front door opened.

Brian came through, his eyes narrowing at her. "What are you doing here?"

Maybe he did have security cameras set up and they were just well hidden.

She gave an easy smile. "Oh, good. I'm glad to see you. I think I might have left my cell phone here last night. I looked everyplace else." She smiled again. "I was hoping somebody might be around to let me in to take a look?"

"Let's see where it rings." He flipped his phone open and pushed a couple of buttons. He had her number in his phone; she'd given it to him the day she was hired.

"If it starts ringing on the bottom of my purse, I'm going to feel really stupid." She reached into the purse to shuffle around and powered off her phone before it could have gone off. Then she stopped searching and turned her attention back to him. "I have no idea where I put that thing."

He waited with his phone to his ear. He wasn't leering at her or staring at her breasts, which was out of character for him. He seemed thoughtful, in fact. Maybe he didn't want to mess with Shep.

"Number unavailable," he said as he put his phone away.

"Great." She grimaced. "The battery probably ran down." She moved toward him. "It might be in the back where I was taking my breaks. Or in the bathroom where I was changing."

He didn't look happy to see her there. In fact, his fat lips had a decidedly angry tilt to them. But then he seemed to make up his mind and stepped aside with a closed look on his face. "Hurry up. We're restocking the liquor. We were just about to leave."

"Thanks." She pushed by him. "Shouldn't take more than five minutes to run through the place."

He locked the door behind them, the metallic click sending a twinge of unease up her spine. He probably just wanted to make sure nobody walked in while they were in the back.

Tank was coming from the direction of the basement. He threw Brian a questioning look. Brian shook his head.

Lilly kept smiling. "Hey, Tank. Can't believe you have to work on Sundays. That bites, man."

Tank didn't comment, just turned around and went back the same way he'd come.

She checked around the stage first, trying

to steal glances at the back hallway. The basement door was open, but she couldn't see anyone coming and going.

Brian watched her wherever she went. "Doesn't look like it's here."

"God, I hope you're wrong. If it's not here, then somebody already took it. I can't afford a new phone. This was a good one. Paid for it from my last gig." She went to the ladies' room next, pushed through the swinging saloon doors in the corner by the jukeboxes.

Brian followed her. "Boyfriend of yours drove you over?"

She checked the stalls. "He's off with his buddies somewhere."

"Them rodeo cowboys never do well. Win a few purses, get hurt, get hooked on drugs, wash up in a couple of years. You could do better." He watched her. "Friendly advice."

She tried to take it lightly, even as more unease settled over her. "It's not like we're getting married. We're just having fun while we're both in town."

Since he wouldn't move, she had to brush by him to get out of the bathroom. "I'll look behind the bar. I put my bag there while I was singing."

Again, he followed, looking as if he was holding back anger. And, again, he seemed to put it away, as if coming to some sort of decision. "Want a beer? On the house."

"Sure." Whatever made him back off for a minute. He was creeping her out, frankly.

She made a show of looking behind the bar while he filled two glasses from the tap and slid one her way.

"Thanks." She gave a deep sigh, then took a gulp. "It's not here, either."

"An iPhone?"

She nodded and drank some more, playing for time. She wanted to see who else was here beyond Brian and Tank. Maybe if she hung around long enough, someone else would come from the back. She was trying to figure out how to offer to help with the stocking without sounding suspicious.

"Those are expensive. Maybe you dropped it in the basement," Brian said.

She thrilled to the suggestion. "Could be." She would have loved it if he let her go down there. She wanted to take a look at what they were really doing here this time of the night.

She drained her glass so fast it would have made a cowboy proud, then headed for the basement door.

Of course, Brian was right behind her once again. "You said you sang in San Antonio before," he was saying as he closed this door, too, behind them.

Even with the light on, the basement was poorly lit, smelling old and dank. She felt as if she was in some old castle dungeon. Goose bumps prickled on her skin.

"Which bar did you say?" he asked.

"Finnegan's." They'd set up a cover for her with the owner, should Brian call for a reference.

She reached the bottom of the stairs, and the main area of the basement opened up in front of her. The space was stacked with sealed, unmarked boxes, close to a hundred of them. When Shep had told her about his meeting down here with Tank, he said the boxes held bottles and were marked with various liquor logos. So this batch was something different.

She moved toward the boxes, making a show of scanning the floor, wishing she could find a way to look into one. She could hear Tank moving things around in one of the rooms. Then he came forward.

"You ever hang out at Finnegan's when you go up to San Antonio?" Brian asked. "Our Lilly used to be their star attraction. How about that?"

Tank watched her darkly as he shrugged. "I've been there."

"Ever see Lilly? You should have told me about her. I would have stolen her away sooner."

Tank shook his head, still watching her. "My brother ain't never heard of her, either, and he hangs out there nearly every night."

Oh, hell. She was beginning to feel as if this was some kind of a setup. She wanted to go back up, but Brian stood at the bottom of the staircase, blocking her way. God, she could have used some fresh air. The musty smell was turning her stomach.

His eyes narrowed at her. "You sure it was Finnegan's?"

"I was only there for a few weeks. Might have been Frankie's." She gave a quick laugh. "Honestly, I was drunk half the time. They gave free beer to the band, too."

Brian didn't seem to think any of that was funny. He watched her stone-faced. "Better look for that phone. I'm ready to get out of here."

Right. She moved around, scanned the ground, trying to ignore the two men and her growing sense of discomfort of being down here with them alone. Not only was she nauseous, she was beginning to feel dizzy, too.

Had to be the chipotle. If Jamie had taken her to a place that gave her food poisoning, she was going to have to revise her good opinion of him.

Tank lumbered back to his work in the room behind her.

But Brian wasn't done questioning her yet,

it seemed, because next he wanted to know "When were you down here that you could have lost the phone?"

"In between sets. Just stuck my head down, really. I was looking for you for something." She covered the area, so she had to give up her pretend search. She made an unhappy face. "I don't think it's here."

"I don't think so, either. But we did find something that might belong to you." He reached into his pocket and pulled out a bug.

"What's that?" She gave a clueless look. Her head was swimming. Could food poisoning hit this fast? "That's not my earring."

The stone-faced look remained. "It's not an earring, and I think you know that."

She didn't ask what it was, just went on with the puzzled look and leaned against the wall as a sudden wave of weakness hit her.

"It's a bug," Brian told her. "We do a sweep every Sunday. There've been only two strangers down here this week, you and your boyfriend."

"Not really my boyfriend. We're just hooking up." She tried to keep it light and did her best not to let him see that she was becoming rapidly incapacitated.

"Who do you work for?"

She gave a nervous laugh as a scared singer might. "You. For now. I mean, I like it here. But

I'm not the long-term-commitment kind. If you change your mind about me, I'll just move on. There are a million small bars in the world."

"I'm going to ask you only one more time. Who do you work for, darling?"

"Are you serious? I don't know what you're talking about. I better get going. I need to find that damn phone." She turned toward the stairs.

But Brian's arms snaked out faster than she'd ever seen him move and he grabbed her arm, yanked her back. "Are you a cop? CBP? Why in hell am I paying all that money if they still send their snoops around, dammit?" He looked openly angry now, even outraged.

He yanked her toward him.

She moved in with a self-defense maneuver, too slow as the basement spun with her. But she would have been free of the bastard the next second, anyway. Except Tank appeared behind her from out of nowhere and his meaty fist came down on the top of her head.

SHE DIDN'T ANSWER her phone. Shep swore as he waited for the interrogation room to free up. He didn't like it when women did the holding-a-grudge thing. Men were so much simpler. Either they were okay with each other, or they settled their differences with their fists and then they were okay. She'd punched him. He let her. Why in hell was she still mad?

The current op was almost over. She blew back into his life for a short time, and she was about to blow back out. Good. He'd be able to focus 100 percent on the job again then. Except the thought made him miserable.

He didn't want her to disappear. At least, he wanted to keep in touch. They couldn't have a romantic relationship, but they could be…something. He needed to talk to her about that.

He shouldn't have made love to her. He knew that, dammit. He shouldn't have made the off-the-cuff marriage offer, either. Obviously, it wasn't what she wanted. A good thing, since he hadn't planned on getting married, ever.

He had no idea what had possessed him to blurt those words out like that. He needed to apologize again. He'd drive by her hotel in the morning, once he was done at the office.

Mo came out of the interrogation room with his guy and led him away. Shep went in with the next.

He clicked on the recorder, noted the man's name and specifics, the date of the interrogation, then started with the questions. "Have you ever met with the Coyote?"

"No, man," the twentysomething kid Lilly

and he had picked up earlier said, looking as tired as Shep felt.

"What do you know about him?"

"He's the boss of everyone, pretty much. You cross him, you disappear." The kid made a slicing motion across his throat. "He'll ground you to dust."

"What's his real name?"

The kid just laughed. "Right, dude. He stopped by my house just to tell me that."

Shep asked another dozen questions. He received no helpful answers, no matter how hard he leaned on the guy.

He stood to stretch his legs. He could have pushed harder, but he was pretty sure the kid was telling the truth. The interrogations were a long shot. It was unlikely that any of the men they'd rounded up had information that would lead directly to the Coyote, but he had to try anyway.

They had the date and they had the place, but what they didn't have was any confirmation and the Coyote's true identity. They couldn't afford any mistakes on this op, any crossed wires, any half-accurate intel. Being able to pick up the bastard for questioning sure would have helped.

Also, even if they caught the tangos sneaking over, who was to say more wouldn't try with the

Coyote's help? The government needed that man in custody and permanently out of business.

"Do you know where Tank is?"

"I don't even know who he is."

Shep kept up with the questions, rotating the men in and out, consulting with Mo in between, until midnight, then went home to catch some sleep before his morning shift started.

On his way to the office, he drove by the hotel. Lilly wasn't in her room, didn't respond to his knocking. She still didn't pick up her phone, either. He walked through the parking garage, but he couldn't find her car.

He went to the front desk, but the guy there didn't remember seeing her going out that morning.

On a hunch, Shep drove by the bar, checked front and back, but the bar was closed and neither Lilly nor her car were there as far as he could tell.

He switched to the monitoring app on his phone and accessed last night's recording from the bar's basement. Since the place had been closed, he didn't expect much, but he wanted to check anyway. They couldn't afford to overlook anything at this stage.

The program was set to skip silence and just go to sound. It wasn't long before Lilly's voice came through on Shep's Bluetooth.

What in hell had she been doing there, alone, without telling him?

Anger punched through him, quickly turning to worry as he heard Brian say, "It's a bug. We do a sweep every Sunday. There've only been two strangers down here this week, you and your boyfriend." Then some more conversation, her protesting her innocence, then the unmistakable sounds of a scuffle.

Then a crunch, as if someone had ground the bug into the cement floor with his heel.

He shut off the recording and called Lilly again. She didn't answer her phone. So as he drove to the office, he kept calling. Until she did pick up, finally.

"Hey, cowboy," she said, tension in her voice, and something else in the way she dragged out the word cowboy. Was she drunk?

"I was about to call you," she said in the same slow drawl.

"Where are you?"

"Out at the rodeo grounds. Listen, I need you out here for a minute."

"What are you doing there? Is everything okay?"

"Nothing to worry about. I'll explain when you get here. Sooner would be better than later. Just hop in that rickety old Mustang of yours and step on the gas. I'll be out by the bull pens."

Oh, hell. He gripped the phone. "I'll be right there. Lilly—"

She hung up before he could have asked any questions.

He drove a souped-up SUV for work and a beat-up pickup for cover. The only Mustang he'd been near lately was Doug Wagner's. Talking about that was her way of warning him there was trouble. And if she didn't simply come out with what that was, it meant she wasn't alone. There was somebody within hearing distance.

He had a good idea who. But why was she at the fairgrounds? And why did she sound drunk at seven in the morning? He didn't like any of that.

He called it in.

"I'm heading out to the rodeo grounds," he told Ryder as he turned his SUV around. "Lilly's there. There's something going on. She got busted at The Armadillo last night. I think Brian and Tank might have her."

"Need backup?"

"Don't know yet." He didn't want to call the guys off the border. He also didn't want to wake Mo unnecessarily since he'd been up all night, working. Keith was still in Mexico, following leads there. Ryder was manning the office, checking satellite images and processing last-minute intel.

"Call me if you need anything," the team leader said.

"Let me get out there and do some recon first."

He drove as fast as he could, bringing up the tourist map of the rodeo grounds on his cell phone. Within a minute, he knew exactly where the bull pens were located.

The rodeo was a weeklong event, starting that afternoon with the opening ceremonies and ending on the following Saturday with the biggest party Pebble Creek had ever seen, supposedly.

The fairgrounds, made into a rodeo arena now, were on the outskirts of town, a sprawling compound of stables and show rings. He didn't pull up into the front parking lot. He didn't pull up into the back one, either. He went to the feed store directly attached to the side of the registration building and parked there.

He checked his guns, the one he kept under his shirt stuck into his waistband at his back and the smaller one that he kept in his right boot. On second thought, he grabbed his other backup gun from the glove compartment and stuck it into his left boot before he got out. He skipped the official entrances and snuck through a hole in the chain-link fence.

Whoever had been listening in while he'd been talking to Lilly on the phone, Shep didn't want them to see him coming. He scanned the area as he walked. The goal was to see them before they saw him.

The opening ceremonies for the rodeo would start at five, after the worst of the heat was done for the day. At the moment only the work crews ambled around the place, cleaning and setting up for the crowds that would come in the evening.

Shep tried to look as if he belonged. He stayed near the perimeter as he made his way to the bull pens in the back. He was going to see what was going on, then call Ryder and report in.

THERE HAD TO be a way out.

Shep would come for her. She hoped. He'd promised to have her back. Well, she needed that now. And she was beginning to appreciate the offer. She wouldn't have been the least upset if he rushed in to save her.

She was locked in a feed bin near the sheep pens at the fairgrounds. There weren't any cracks in the heavy plastic box, so she couldn't see anything. Lilly could hear the sheep, though, and a dog barking now and then. She breathed deeply, wrinkling her nose against the smells that surrounded her, and did her best to keep from passing out again.

Could have been worse. They could have put

her in with the bulls. She was gagged with a nasty length of rag and bound hands and feet, wedged in between feed sacks. Must have been a hundred degrees. She could barely breathe.

She shifted, testing her restraints once again but, like before, they didn't give.

She couldn't remember much about getting here. She'd been fading in and out. She remembered Tank throwing a bucket of cold water into her face. He'd forced her to take that call from Shep, then let her fade out again.

How long ago was that?

Could Shep be here already?

And if he was, how would he find her?

She needed to think, but her brain was still frustratingly slow. She felt beyond tired, as if she would die if she didn't sleep a little more. She bit the inside of her cheek so the pain would jolt her back awake.

She could have kicked herself for letting Brian and Tank take her as easily as they had. She'd been so focused on Brian, she hadn't noticed Tank sneaking up behind her until it'd been too late. A rookie mistake.

She shook her head to clear the fog.

She didn't make rookie mistakes, dammit. Her stomach rolled.

And the answer hit her, ridiculously obvious in hindsight. Images flashed into her mind,

Brian turning with her glass as he'd slid the beer down the bar to her.

She hadn't been feeling so out of focus because of food poisoning from the chipotle like she'd stupidly thought at the time. Brian had put something in her beer.

He had the drug ready behind the bar, slipped it into the drink with practiced ease, handed it to her without batting an eye. Had he done that to other women before? She wouldn't have been surprised.

But he'd messed with the wrong girl this time.

She pushed the gag out of her mouth as best she could and stretched her neck to rub the rag on her shoulder, trying to push it down a little so she could breathe easier. Minutes ticked by before she succeeded.

She gulped in air that smelled like sheep and manure, then refocused on freeing her hands. She didn't succeed any better this time, but when she bent to her ankles, she managed to untie the rope that bound them together, even if she broke nearly every nail in the process.

She did her best to stretch her legs and get her circulation going. Being able to move a little more freely felt nice. Okay, what else could she do?

The storage container wasn't tall enough for her to stand. She got on her knees and rammed the lid with her back. It rattled, but nothing gave. They'd probably padlocked it. She rammed it again anyway.

And then someone kicked it from the outside, hard, scaring her.

She banged with her bound fists. "Let me out of here! Let me out!"

"Shut up," Tank thundered.

The sheep bleated as something motorized started up somewhere nearby and came closer. Then the container rattled and lifted suddenly, and she fell to her side as her body shifted.

What was that? A forklift?

The feed box was definitely moving, which set her head swimming again. She nearly lost her chipotle dinner before the container was set down. And then she heard something slam with a metallic clang.

She had no idea what that was. "Tank? Don't do this!"

A different, louder motor started up next, the ground suddenly vibrating under her.

She was in the back of a truck; the stark realization hit her. They could take her anywhere, across the border even. "Tank?"

He didn't answer. Maybe he was up front, ready to drive her to wherever they planned on executing her and getting rid of her body. Her muscles clenched, cold sweat beading on her forehead despite the heat.

In case Shep was anywhere within hearing distance, she screamed his name at the top of her lungs. "Shep!"

There was nothing in this world she wanted as much as she wanted to see him again.

Chapter Ten

Three men loitered around the bull pens, talking and spitting tobacco juice in the dust now and then. No sign of Lilly anywhere, as far as Shep could tell. Then Tank and Brian lumbered forward from behind a corrugated-steel building that stood between the bull pens and the sheep, and joined the other three.

Shep pulled behind a row of portable toilets and called Ryder to give him a status update. "Yes, five men that I can see, including Tank and Brian. I think they have Lilly stashed here somewhere." He peeked out to scan the building.

"We can lock the whole place down."

Ryder scanned the sprawling area. They probably couldn't. At least not on their own. The fairgrounds were pretty big and fairly porous. The best they could do in a hurry would be to ask for help from local law enforcement and whatever security was already here for the rodeo, although the security guys were probably undertrained rent-a-cops at best. And there was no telling how many friends Brian and Tank had among them.

The bastards had to have chosen the fairgrounds for a reason. Because they were familiar here, because they had backup here, because they probably did some kind of illegal business from here.

Drugs, guns and human trafficking had all been linked to Pebble Creek in the past couple of weeks. One by one, the leaders of the local crime organization had been taken down by Shep and his team. It looked as if Brian was trying to step into the power vacuum to fill it.

Shep didn't care about any of that right now. All he wanted was to see Lilly safe.

"I don't know if we can do a full lockdown fast enough," he told Ryder.

Keith was still in Mexico. Mo and Ray were on border patrol and should probably stay there. "A couple of guys might be able to quickly run through the place and pinpoint her location, take Brian and his goons in, if it's just the five of them. We can sort them out later."

"I can be there with Jamie in twenty minutes. And I'll call Bree to send over whoever she fully trusts from her department. I'll call Grace, too. That's all I can do in a hurry."

"It'll be enough." He scanned the area and

was planning the search already. "You think Grace will come?"

"It's not even a question. Of course she will. Do what you can, but try to keep a low profile until we get there. Don't engage the men. Just see if you can narrow down Lilly's location."

Okay. More than anything, he was glad for Grace. Lilly had sounded strange on the phone. As if she'd been drunk *or* hazy from blood loss—the possibility occurred to him suddenly and set his teeth on edge.

Grace Cordero was Ryder's fiancée, a tough former army medic. If Tank had hurt Lilly— which Shep didn't even want to think about— Grace would come in handy. She was as good with injuries as she was with hand-to-hand combat.

"Thanks, man."

He hung up then skirted the bull pens, ducking from cover to cover, making his way over to the corrugated-steel building. They had the sheep pens behind that, and a truck parked at the far end. Nobody sat behind the wheel for the moment, so he decided to investigate the building first. The truck didn't look as if it was going anywhere in a hurry.

He went around and kept in cover, snuck forward from the side when nobody was looking, then kept behind a row of baled hay. He slipped through the door then ducked into the shadows to his left and waited until his eyes adjusted to the semidarkness, trying to see if he was alone in there.

He couldn't see anyone. Nor could he hear any voices in here.

They had stations set up to groom the sheep, piles of feed, everything the ranchers would need to take care of and show their livestock. The piles of supplies everywhere made it difficult to scan the place fully from where he stood, so he had to go check behind stacks of feed bags and equipment.

The good news was that all the mess also provided him with cover. He moved silently and stayed low as he stole forward, little by little. Lilly could be tied up and gagged, hidden just about anywhere in here.

His phone vibrated in his pocket. A text message from Grace Cordero. I'm here. Where R U?

Corrugatd steel bldng by sheep, he texted back.

She'd come a lot faster than he'd expected. Then again, she was a veterinarian in her postarmy career. Maybe she'd already been out at the fairgrounds, taking care of some sick animal. Whatever the reason for her speedy arrival, the important thing was that she was here. Shep moved forward.

Voices sounded behind him, at the entrance. He hurried to the end of a row of feed sacks and stuck his head out enough to see. Brian and Tank were coming back in.

The good news was, they might lead him to Lilly.

The bad news was, they had a couple of sheepdogs following them.

And, of course, the dogs sniffed the ground and caught his scent pretty fast. They barked as they ran straight to Shep.

They didn't attack, friendly as anything, playing greeting committee, blissfully unaware that they'd just given away his location.

Tank and Brian spread out and moved toward him. He didn't want to play hide-and-seek. He wanted Lilly. Shep drew his weapon and stepped out into the open.

He aimed at Tank while keeping an eye on Brian. "Where is she?"

Brian lifted his hands immediately and stopped next to a workstation, pulled closer to it to use it as cover if needed. Tank didn't look scared. Shep knew Tank usually carried a weapon and therefore kept his gun aimed at him rather than Brian.

"Stop where you are." He dropped the goofy Pennsylvania rodeo-cowboy act altogether and went for this commando voice and stance. "Hands in the air. On your stomach, on the ground."

But Tank just shot him a fearsome dark look and kept moving forward, his mouth set into a narrow line, anger flaring in his eyes. He reached his right hand toward his back.

Shep aimed for his shoulder.

But before he could squeeze the trigger, there was a sudden movement to his left and something punched him in the neck.

What the hell? It stung. A burning sensation began spreading down his arm.

He pulled out the dart as his gaze switched to Brian, who was holding a tranquilizer gun. He'd stopped at that workstation for a reason, Shep realized too late.

The man gave a cocky chuckle. "Just got it a few weeks ago. I thought it might be nice to have in case a bull goes crazy during training. I put too much money into some of my boys to let them get hurt."

Shep swung his weapon toward him. He meant to, in any case. His arm sagged instead, his knees buckling. That stuff worked fast. That was the point, of course, if anyone had an angry bull charging at them.

The average rodeo bull weighed close to two thousand pounds. Even as hard as Shep fought, the tranquilizer took him down in seconds.

ON HER KNEES again, Lilly kept ramming her back into the top of the storage container, still hoping to break through the heavy plastic.

At first, she could hear other cars. The truck had driven through town. But then the ride got bumpier and the sounds of the road stopped. They were on rougher ground somewhere, off-roading it.

Her entire back ached and was probably bruised, but she didn't care. She had a fair idea where they were going: somewhere isolated. And she had an ever better idea of what the men would do when they got there.

They probably thought her an undercover, overeager border agent. They needed to make her disappear. Lord knew the possibilities for that were endless in the South Texas border-lands. She knew who they were and she knew their dirty business. They simply couldn't afford to let her live.

She alternated pushing with her shoulders then lying on her back and kicking with her feet.

She had no idea how long she had before they would stop, but she meant to break free before that. Her best chance for escape was if she could either open the back door and jump from the truck without them noticing or, at least, stand ready by the door and jump on them from above as they came to get her. She'd have the element of surprise.

If she could knock them down, if she could grab a gun—

A pained groan outside her dark box interrupted that optimistic fantasy, startling her. She stilled and listened.

Nothing.

Maybe she'd only imagined it.

But just as she was about to start her efforts again, the groan repeated. This was no sheep they might have put in the back of the truck with her. The sound was decidedly human.

Friend or foe was the question. She meant to find out the answer. She banged her fist on the side of the crate. "Hey! Who is that?"

Even if it was Tank, maybe she could talk him into opening the lid for a second. If she could somehow grab his weapon...

But no response came.

She banged again. "I'm in here. Help me!"

Another minute of silence, then a rusty, croaking sound that might have been "Lilly?"

The familiar voice flooded her with relief. "Shep? I'm stuck in here. Can you help?"

"Give me a minute."

He sounded strange, slow and dazed. Was he injured? Maybe they'd beaten him before they'd tossed him in the back of the truck with her.

That would explain why he hadn't responded to her banging before. Maybe he'd been beaten unconscious. "Are you okay?"

A moment of silence followed, then, "What are you doing in there?"

All the frustration inside her surged to the front. "Getting a pedicure. What do you think?"

"Okay," he said after a minute. "Move away from the lid."

She flattened herself to the bottom of the container and pulled some feed bags on top of her.

Was he going to try to shoot the padlock off? She didn't think Brian and Tank would have let him keep his weapon. They'd certainly taken everything she had.

Bang!

Then suddenly the lid popped up, and Shep was there, gripping it with one hand while holding a fire extinguisher with the other. He blinked at her slowly, looking out-of-this-world stoned, his irises wide, his movements not altogether coordinated.

"When did Brian give *you* a roofie?" She sat up, grateful to be able to breathe freely at last, every muscle in her body aching. Her clothes stuck to her with sweat, but she was uninjured, miraculously. She climbed out, with his help.

"Bull tranquilizer," he said, his eyes glazed

over. "I pulled it out, so I don't think I got the full dosage."

"Thank God." The full dosage might have killed him. "Brian slipped me a roofie," she told him.

He scanned her with thunder on his face, reaching for her hands.

"Not for that purpose," she said to ease his obvious worries. "Just so they could move me around easier." But his touch felt nice, so she didn't pull away for a few seconds.

Enough daylight filtered in through the cracks under the door, and a small hole in the roof so she could scan the back of the truck. Other than the crate, the fire extinguisher and the two of them, it was empty. "Now what?"

"Now we escape. Do you trust me?"

"Yes." She wasn't sure it was entirely smart, but she did trust him anyway. He'd come for her. He didn't leave her to her fate, he didn't abandon her—he came.

Since he was bound, hands and feet, she helped him break free, then he helped untie her wrists.

She rubbed her bruised skin before shaking off the minor injury. "Good to go."

But even as she said that, the truck began to slow, coming to a full stop after a minute. Then they heard car doors slamming and two men arguing in Spanish.

"*¡Idiota!* Why didn't you fill up the tank?"

"The boss said to hurry. Didn't want to stop before we hit the border. The next gas station is at the factory. I thought we'd make it."

The other one swore. "Now what do we do?"

"Walk?"

"To the factory? *¡Zurramato!*"

Lilly stayed still and silent as she shot a questioning look at Shep.

Dumb ass. He mouthed the translation as the conversation continued outside.

"And the ones in the back?" one of the men asked. "The boss said the Coyote would want to talk to them."

"The boss also said to shoot them if we run into any trouble."

"We could get good money for the *chica* down south."

"You want to carry her on your back?"

The other one swore. "Let's do it, then, so we can get going." He swore again, more vehemently this time. "It's still a waste just to shoot her."

"You do what you want with her first, but I'm not waiting for you. Your business if you want to die out here."

A threatening growl escaped Shep's throat

as he stepped up to the truck's back door, the fire extinguisher lifted and ready. Lilly moved next to him, going down into a crouch. Whatever she had to do, she wasn't going to become entertainment for those two bastards out there.

The roofie had worn off. She was ready. They wouldn't find her quite as easy prey this time around.

Then the doors popped open, revealing two men holding guns. One gave a surprised shout, but that was that. Shep slammed the bottom of the fire extinguisher into his face, while Lilly vaulted onto the other guy, knocking him to the ground, driving her elbow into his solar plexus.

Dust flew up around them as he tried to roll her, but her self-defense skills put her on top in quick order. All good, except for the damned gun trapped between them.

The man grinned into her face. He shifted his arm just an inch or so, but that would be enough. *"Hasta la vista, puta."*

She tried to grab the gun, but just as the top of her fingers reached metal, he pulled the trigger.

She yanked her other elbow down hard at the same split second, hitting his forearm. Then she froze, waiting to see which one of them got hit.

"Lilly?" Shep was grabbing her and pulling her up.

She moved with him. That had to be a good

sign, right? She didn't feel pain, but she wouldn't necessarily. The adrenaline surge after a major injury often came with a minute of reprieve.

There was blood on her, but there was blood on the man staring up at them, too. His eyes filled with surprise before they went dull and lifeless in just seconds.

Shep shook her. "Lilly."

She rolled her shoulders. "I'm okay."

He yanked her to him and wrapped his arms around her so tightly, she could barely breathe. She let herself accept the comfort for a few seconds. Then her gaze caught on the second man over Shep's shoulder, on the ground behind him, blood pooling under his head, the dry ground drinking it in.

She pulled away.

Shep followed her gaze, his expression darkening. "Hit him too hard." He swore. "I misjudged it. Didn't know how good my muscles were working with all the drugs in my system."

The men were both dead, beyond questioning.

For the first time, she looked around and examined the landscape. They were in the middle of nowhere, nothing but desert and cacti as far as the eye could see. "I'm pretty sure we're in Mexico."

Shep nodded, gathering up the guns and giving her one of them. Then he searched the men's pockets. "Enrique Lopez and Gus Garcia." He considered the lifeless men with an aggravated look on his face. "The names say anything to you?"

She shook her head. "Brian's hired goons, no doubt. I don't remember seeing them at the bar, though. But this all ties to him. They probably worked at one of his other businesses."

Shep took a cell phone off the guy he'd taken down, flipped it open and grimaced. "No reception whatsoever." He shoved the phone into his pocket anyway.

She bent to search her guy, found his phone, but the bullet had damaged it. It was as dead as its owner, although Lilly regretted the owner's death a lot less.

"Doesn't look like we'll be making any calls." Shep scanned the horizon. "We're going to have to walk. Let's see what we can find in the cab."

She moved up front with him, but nothing waited for them there beyond a bag of nacho chips and a few cans of beer. Not terribly helpful, since alcohol only hastened dehydration. They grabbed them anyway.

She stepped back down to the ground and walked toward the road. Standing around in this heat wasn't going to do them any favors. The sooner they got somewhere, the sooner they could get out of the sun and call the office.

She nodded toward the flat, endless dirt road, little more than tire tracks in the desert, the way home. "Back the way we've come?"

But Shep gestured in the opposite direction. "I want to check that hill first. The phone might work on top of that. Or we might see a village or this factory they talked about. Although, from the way they were talking, that might be a couple of miles from here."

"If we can make a call, we can come back here and wait in the shade of the truck until Ryder sends a chopper."

They walked side by side at a brisk pace, keeping an eye out for traffic, but the road was dead. Seemed like a seasonal dirt road, out of the way. Not impossible that it was only used by smugglers.

"This is bad," she said.

"Not too bad. We'll manage."

She shook her head. "That wasn't what I meant. Today is September thirtieth. Looks like the National Guard will be coming in tonight. And we're stuck in the middle of nowhere."

"We make a good team. We'll figure something out together," he said with grim determination and picked up speed.

SHEP SLIPPED THE phone back into his pocket. Standing at the top of the hill did not, in fact, help with reception whatsoever. But they did see a lonely ranch in the distance with some goats and a horse grazing on some sparse grasses behind the fence.

"There we go," he said and started out that way. Then he paused and looked back at Lilly. "How are you doing?"

"Fine. Better to move toward water and shade than sit here and fry to death." Her kissable mouth was set into a determined line. She wasn't the type to give up and roll over.

He admired that about her. She looked worse for wear, her hair and clothes a mess, yet to him, she was still the most beautiful woman in the world.

They walked side by side in the heat. His head was finally clear of the tranquilizer drug, but it left behind a pounding headache that the relentless sun wasn't helping.

"Why didn't you tell me you were going to the bar?" he asked. Before he'd tried the phone, they'd been talking about how she'd ended up with Brian and Tank. Anger stiffened his muscles every time he thought of those bastards. She could have been killed.

"I don't need a babysitter."

"It's called working with a partner. Ever heard of this new thing called a *team?*"

She shrugged. "Heard of it. Don't like it."

"Don't FBI agents work with partners? You had to have one over the years."

"I've worked alone for the last couple of months. The last partner I had... Anyway, I was dragging my feet accepting another. I volunteered for this job partially because it was a solo mission. It's easier when you only have yourself to consider."

He didn't entirely disagree with that. He'd spent most of his time with the SDDU on lonewolf ops overseas. Yet he would have been lying if he said he hadn't come to like his current team and the way they worked together here. "What happened to your last partner?"

"She was shot to death by her boyfriend. He was drunk and jealous." She shook her head. "You go to work every day, deal with the worst kind of criminals, put your life on the line, then you go home where you should be able to relax and some scumbag puts a bullet through your head in your sleep." Her lips flattened.

That sounded rough. "Not all partnerships work."

"Yeah." She walked on. "They were poison for each other. She couldn't live with him, couldn't live without him. They tore each other down pretty badly. Maybe I should have seen it coming. I knew how it was between them."

He wasn't exactly an expert on relationships.

He lived for his job for the most part, his brief hookups few and far between.

They walked in silence for a while before she added, "People who are supposed to love you and have your back will let you down. They abandon you or worse. You don't trust anyone but yourself and you don't get hurt."

Her own life experiences bore that out, so the sentiment was difficult to argue with, but he did anyway. "Sometimes. And sometimes people who are supposed to love you do love you and have your back. There are good people. We just mostly deal with the bad in our jobs."

She blew the hair out of her face. "I think deep down I know that. But I still can't trust people. Tell me that's not stupid."

"I don't think anyone could go through what you went through and not have abandonment issues."

"I was starting to trust you. Back when. That's why I ran away. I figured I better get out of there before you punched me in the face or something and proved yourself to be a fake."

Hell. What was he supposed to say to that?

She didn't wait for him to speak. "You're not a fake."

"Thanks." The quiet declaration touched him.

They walked on, side by side, cutting through the desert together. He didn't see any vehicles around the house, or any people. Didn't look as if anybody was home.

"When I say I have your back," he said after a while, "I don't mean because I don't think you can handle things. I just mean, I want to be there for you because you're important to me."

She turned to him and stared for a long second. "I am?"

"You're the first woman I ever proposed to."

She turned away. "You didn't mean it."

Didn't he? "I had no idea what to say." He paused. "What happened between us, what we shared…I don't think it happens to people every day. I don't want it to never happen between us again. I do care about you, and I do want to protect you. Hell, I want things I haven't even dared to dream about before now. I want you to let me in."

She stared at him. "It'll take getting used to."

"We have time." Warmth spread through his chest. This was what he wanted. She was what he wanted. He'd been a fool to try to keep her at arm's length. He couldn't do that. Not when he was falling for her.

The realization made his mouth go dry.

"We have time," he said again, because he didn't think he could say what he was thinking.

"If we don't get shot in the head or die of dehydration here first," she observed wryly.

"There's always the beer." He lifted the cans.

She grinned. "Yeah, die drunk, die happy."

"Beats dying sad." He grinned back at her, relieved that the conversation was lightening up a little.

They nearly reached the corral with the lone horse when she said, "I do trust you. And I want to trust Jamie. I want to trust the rest of the team."

"They all like you." He made a face. "A little too much for my taste, actually. And they trust you, which is a miracle, considering you're an FBI outsider."

And I more than like you, he wanted to say. He wanted to tell her that their connection went beyond attraction and great sex. He wasn't sure if a relationship could ever work, but he wanted to try anyway, even if it would be long-distance and they could spend frustratingly little time together. Because he could no longer picture going back to a life devoid of Lilly.

But before he could find the words, the smile slid off her face. She grew somber and searched his gaze as she stopped walking.

He didn't like that look. "What is it?"

She brushed her hair out of her face. "I'm not here just to observe the team."

"You're here to provide help if possible."

"That and more." She looked away.

A cold feeling sneaked up his spine. "What more?"

"I'm to make a recommendation when I get back. About whether the SDDU should be able to operate on U.S. soil."

The sense of betrayal that washed over him was staggering. He stepped back from her. "You're here to spy on us and give bureaucrats ammunition against us to shut us down?"

"It's not like that."

"Sure sounds like that from where I'm standing." He turned from her and walked away. A hard knot replaced all the warm, fuzzy feelings in his chest.

He should have known better. He'd known that his job and relationships didn't mix. What the hell had he been thinking? She'd been sent to spy on them!

Did the Colonel know about this? He couldn't have. He would have told the team.

"What we do here is important, dammit," he called back. "Maybe we're a little less politically correct than the domestic agencies. Maybe we've brought in some rougher battlefield tactics. But the enemy we fight doesn't exactly play by the rules of polite society, in case you haven't noticed."

That Lilly wouldn't understand that cut him to the quick. He turned away from her again and kept going. Maybe she wasn't who he thought she was. Maybe he'd been an utter fool about her. Sure looked like it.

He walked up to the ramshackle house. He didn't want to fight with her right now. Not here. So he called out a couple of loud hellos, but the house seemed empty. Only some mutts came running, barking their heads off. They calmed right down when he offered a handful of tortilla chips.

He tossed more onto the ground then walked up to the front door. A crumpled piece of paper was tacked to the wood, with a few lines written on it in Spanish. It was a notice to drop the feed in the barn, as whoever lived here had gotten called into work and wouldn't be home until later.

Shep knocked anyway. No response came.

"Hello?" He tried the door, found it locked, so he kicked it in.

They needed water. He already knew they wouldn't find a phone. No phone lines led to the place. Out here in the middle of nowhere, there wouldn't be any utilities.

He found some food, goat jerky and goat cheese. He took some of that, while Lilly filled up four empty soda bottles with water. He left the beer on the table for partial payment, and the pesos and dollars they'd found on the men who'd kidnapped them, then went outside to look for a saddle.

The horse was their only hope at this stage.

He found the saddle in the barn, next to the feed that had apparently been delivered already.

"We should keep going forward rather than back," he told Lilly, who came into the barn after him. "Riding through abandoned borderlands in this heat will be slow going and it'll take forever. Let's see if we can find this factory."

She held his gaze. "I'm sorry. I'm just doing my job, like everyone else."

"I don't want to fight about that right now. We can discuss it when we're home and the terrorists are in custody."

She nodded.

He headed out of the barn. "We'll keep going south. We can make a call from the factory."

"Do you think the Coyote is there?"

He shrugged. The men had talked about getting gas for the truck at the factory, and also about taking Lilly and Shep to the Coyote, but it didn't mean that the Coyote was at the factory. They might have been talking about stopping at the factory for gas on their way to the Coyote somewhere farther south.

He made sure the horse had enough to drink before he saddled the animal, not that it looked thrilled with the idea of going for a ride in this heat.

Lilly held the bridle and she patted the horse's neck to calm him. "You ride?"

"Reluctantly."

She raised an eyebrow. "Your cover was being a rodeo cowboy."

"It was the first thing we could come up with under short notice." He looked her over. "How about you?"

She gave a flat smile. "I was fostered on a horse farm for a while. I ride like the wind."

"Fine. You'll sit in front, then, and steer the beast."

She went up first, in a fluid move.

He wasn't as graceful, but he made it up behind her.

Okay, they were close. Way too close. He'd never ridden double before. The way her behind rubbed against him was pretty indecent. Even if it felt damned good. Too good. He hoped their ride would be short.

He didn't dare put his arms around her slim waist as she spurred the horse to move. He didn't want to make things worse. He was still mad at her, dammit. He didn't want to want a woman who would spy on him and his team.

But other than her being fitted tightly against him, he didn't mind the backseat. It left his hands free for his gun, in case they ran into trouble.

Which, of course, they did.

Chapter Eleven

They'd only ridden maybe a mile from the ranch when they ran into a heavily armed posse.

Lilly's best guess was that the two pickups full of men had been sent to find out what had happened to the truck that hadn't arrived on time. She and Shep were armed with handguns, while the others carried semiautomatics.

She stopped the horse as they were surrounded within seconds, all guns aimed at them. Then she raised her hands. Defeat was a foregone conclusion.

Shep swore behind her.

"Live to fight another day," she whispered as she let her weapon drop to the ground. The two of them dying in the middle of the desert would serve no purpose.

She would have dearly liked to kick Shep, maybe, but she didn't want him dead. All this time, he'd been telling her that she could trust him. So she'd trusted him enough to tell him about her job. Did he appreciate it? Hell, no. There was absolutely no rhyme or reason to him.

Even now, was he doing the sensible thing and surrendering? Of course not.

He held on to his gun as one of the men, probably the leader, yelled at him. If he squeezed off a single shot, the next second they'd both be riddled with bullets.

"Think of the upside," she said under her breath. "I think we're about to meet the illustrious Coyote."

If these men wanted them dead, they would have shot as soon as they'd gotten within range. That they hadn't could only mean that they'd been ordered to bring Shep and Lilly in.

Shep swore again, but tossed his weapon onto the parched ground at last. "I really hope we're not going to regret this."

She had to wonder when the next second the men ran forward and pulled them from the horse, tied them up and shoved them into one of the pickups. They drove back in the direction they'd come from, their captives lying on the truck bed while the men sat on the wooden planks that rimmed the back.

Her bruised back didn't enjoy the ride. At least she wasn't gagged this time, a small mercy she was grateful for. And the men shaded them somewhat so they weren't lying in full sun, either.

Shep asked in Spanish where they were going, but they ignored him, until he insisted on an answer too loudly and one of the men kicked him in the mouth, splitting his lip.

"Quit it," she whispered. If they were to survive, they had to stick together. "This isn't going to get us anywhere."

He glared at her, probably still upset with her because she was doing her job. So unfair.

She turned her head from him and tried to see out but couldn't as she was ringed by scruffy, sweaty men. Some looked bored, staring ahead at the road. Two leered at her openly.

They didn't go far. Less than half an hour passed before they entered some kind of a factory complex and the pickup pulled into a loading bay. The first thing she saw when they dragged her out of the back of the pickup were giant reams of paper.

An impeccably dressed man stood by the sliding metal doors that led inside. He was Asian, middle-aged.

She exchanged a look with Shep.

The man's identity wasn't difficult to guess, although she hadn't met him before. But there was only one Chinese bigwig who had a paper factory on this side of the border this close to Pebble Creek: Yo Tee.

The men dragged their prisoners over to him for inspection.

"Who do you work for?" he asked with a slight accent as he looked them over.

Neither of them said a word.

"You work for border patrol, no? How much you know?"

Of course, he'd want to know that to see if his plans had been compromised.

Again, they remained silent. Lilly was scanning the place from the corner of her eye, noting avenues of escape and making an inventory of how many people they would have to deal with. She was pretty sure Shep was doing the same.

An annoyed frown flashed across Yo Tee's face. "Not answering questions very impolite." He tsked. "Take them in the back, Carlos." He turned away. "Bring them to me when they ready to talk. Sooner better than later."

By the time the men shoved them up the steps, Yo Tee had disappeared. A wide hallway lined with forklifts greeted them inside. A storage area sprawled straight ahead, but they didn't go there. They headed down a narrow hallway on their right, boots slapping on the cement floor.

Several doors lined the hallway, all of them closed. They were taken to the last one. One of the men unlocked the door and shoved them in, then the door banged shut behind them. The key turned in the lock.

Her gaze flew to the half-naked man on the floor in the far corner, all bloodied. Cuts covered his body, not a good sign for the newcomers.

He didn't look Mexican. He had fair skin and blondish hair, matted with blood.

Shep went to crouch next to him. "Hey, are you all right?"

The man moaned in response. He looked as if Yo Tee's men pulled any punches.

Shep glanced back at her and she shot him a helpless look. There was absolutely nothing they could have done to help the poor guy.

Shep must have come to the same conclusion, because he turned from the man to scan the rest of the space. "We don't have much time. They'll be coming in a minute."

"Where did they go?"

"To get their tools, probably."

She so didn't want to think about what those tools might be. Judging from the man on the ground, they would be sharp. She'd just as soon not see them up close and personal. "We need to get out."

Shep was already sitting and untying the rope from his ankles. She did the same, then helped him untie his hands and he helped with hers like before, as if this was their usual routine.

The door was locked. She tried it anyway, grabbed the knob and shook it hard. Nothing gave.

Shep nodded toward a small window high up on the wall. "How about that?"

The narrow opening had two metal bars crossing each other but no glass, probably to let some air in. It didn't look too promising as an avenue of escape. For one, the window was too high up the wall. And the bars had been built directly into the brick.

But since she had no other suggestions, she moved that way. "Let me see."

Shep stood by the wall, cupped his hands and gave her a boost. Once she was standing on his wide shoulders, she could reach the opening. Unfortunately, it seemed as narrow up close as it had looked from below.

"You're not going to fit," she said, giving him the bad news first as she rattled the bars. "But I will."

"Then you must go," he said without hesitation.

"I'll climb out through here, then come around and set you free." She rattled the bars again. They were old and no longer tight in the brick, but she couldn't rip them out bare-handed. "I need something sharp and hard."

He swayed under her for a few seconds then passed up his belt. "Use the buckle."

She attacked the mortar between the bricks with the sharp square of brass, and it did work, the dried-out material crumbling. The only question was, could she get it all done before the men came back?

She went at the task with all her strength, knowing they had minutes at best. The bottom end of the perpendicular bar came out, the rest wobbled. To free them one by one would be too much work, she realized. They weren't going to make it doing things that way.

"Loop the belt around the bar," Shep called up, apparently having come to the same realization.

She did, catching on at once what he wanted. She looped the belt then jumped to the ground from his shoulders.

They grabbed the end of the belt together and yanked hard. The bar flew out of the wall on the third try, Shep catching it with the reflexes of a superhero before it could have clattered to the ground and given them away.

Then she was on his shoulders again, pulling herself up and looking out.

She was in some kind of a ventilation shaft

surrounded by four brick walls. The shaft had no exit on the bottom, but was open to the sky above.

She glanced back at Shep. "I'm going up. Try not to get into any trouble until I get back."

He looked up from weighing the iron bars, probably testing them to use as a weapon. "Be careful. Don't take unnecessary chances. Getting a call through to Ryder at the office is more important than coming back for me."

"I'm planning on doing both." And she got started right away.

She had to play with the angle to fit her shoulders through the opening. She felt his hands grabbing her feet, giving her support and pushing, helping her up and out. Then she was up all the way, outside, standing in the opening.

The drop to the ground was about fifteen feet, not a big deal, but she'd be trapped down there. The way up was a lot more difficult, at least thirty feet, and with nothing to hang on to but minuscule grooves between bricks that could crumble at any moment beneath her shoes and fingers.

And she had to rush. If the men came back, they could easily figure out where she'd gone. Them shooting up through the window would be like shooting fish in a barrel with her stuck in a tight, boxed-in space with nowhere to hide.

She brought her right foot up, wedged the sole of her shoe into the gap between two bricks and tested it, putting her weight on it little by little. It held, but she didn't shift her full weight forward; she kept some on her hands. Then came the other foot, then moving hands, never letting just one limb carry her full weight, but always two and preferably three. Up she went step by step, reach by reach.

There were other windows opening to the ventilation shaft, small like the one she'd just exited. All barred so she couldn't climb in. One she passed opened to a storage room, another to an empty office. At least there was nobody in either room, so nobody spotted her as she climbed.

Still, she barely dared breathe until she reached the roof and pulled herself up. No gunshots or shouting had come from below, so they hadn't discovered her missing yet, but that could change at any second.

She wasted no time and ran across the roof. She needed a gun, a phone and to get back to Shep before they beat him bloody.

She dashed to the edge of the roof, flattened herself and looked down at the same loading dock they'd come through. There were several trucks waiting for their loads. To grab one and drive away didn't even occur to her. She was going nowhere without Shep.

Even as she thought that, three guys came from inside and began loading one of the trucks, ending any possibility of her climbing down on this side. She pulled back and hurried to another spot, around the corner.

An abandoned courtyard stretched down below, stacked with rusty equipment. She spotted an open window directly below her. Perfect. Unless, of course, she slipped and got impaled on the machinery on the ground. Best not to think about that right now.

She pushed everything but her next move out of her mind and lowered herself next to the window. She carefully peeked in from the side. But there was nobody in there, thank God. She pulled herself over and in, dropped to the tile floor and stayed in a crouch for a second.

That had been nerve-racking. She participated in regular training sessions and worked out daily, but didn't exactly do a lot of rock climbing.

Thinking of Shep, she didn't pause for long. In a few seconds she was moving again, through the empty office, sticking her head into the hallway. There was one more door to her right, at the end of the hallway, a security door that looked as if it was made of reinforced steel.

On her other side she could see four more regular wooden doors toward the stairs. Those, too, all remained closed. She stepped out and hurried that way, glad that the doors had no glass, so even if there were people inside the offices, she wouldn't be seen. Unless, of course, they exited. But nobody did, and she made her way to the staircase safely.

But as she looked down the empty staircase, she could hear angry shouting coming from below.

They'd just figured out that she'd escaped. That should gain Shep a few minutes of a break, while the men all ran off looking for her.

She needed a gun, but for that she would have to catch one of the men. Or… She turned to the steel-reinforced door. *A top-floor office with top security. Yo Tee?*

One way to find out.

She stole back down the hallway to that last door and tried the knob. She wasn't that surprised to find that it gave under the pressure of her hand. Yo Tee wouldn't expect an attack in his own stronghold.

She shoved the door open and rushed in, counting on the element of surprise, and found herself in a small entryway with another door directly opposite her. A guy with an assault rifle guarded the space.

"Who the hell are you?" he asked in Spanish and lurched forward.

She started with a kick to the man's middle, ducked when he tried to bash her face in with the butt of the gun. "Where is the Coyote?" She turned and kicked higher, at his arm this time, but he held the weapon tightly and didn't drop it, dammit.

Instead, he pulled back to aim it at her, but she stepped right in with a hard punch to his solar plexus. Then a quick second punch to his stomach again. He bent forward at that, and she used the advantage to bring her knee up.

His nose broke with a satisfying crunch, spraying blood on her, the least of her concerns. She didn't even slow down as she grabbed his gun and whacked him in the back of the head, sending him sprawling onto the floor. She did hesitate, but only for a second, before bending and breaking his neck. She didn't want him reviving and attacking her from behind.

She kept the gun and rushed the inner door. This one was locked. But it wasn't steel. A good roundhouse kick next to the lock took care of it, and she, carried by momentum, fell through the opening.

She was in a sprawling office this time, Yo Tee coming through yet another door in the back, drying his hands. He'd probably been in his private bathroom. He froze as she pointed the rifle at him.

"Freeze."

He did. But he didn't look scared. "You think this over," he told her. "Whoever you are, I make you rich beyond your dreams. I don't think you understand who I am and what I do for the people who help me."

"Put your hands in the air."

He gave a superior smile. "You American law enforcement. You have no jurisdiction here."

She nodded at the rifle. "This gives me enough jurisdiction for the moment. Hands in the air."

He complied, keeping the smile on his face even as his gaze hardened to frozen steel.

She stepped closer and searched him, took a small pistol off him and stuck it into her waistband. "Don't move."

She sidled over to the desk and lifted the phone, dialed Jamie's cell, her gaze darting back and forth between the phone and Yo Tee.

Jamie picked up on the third ring.

"Hey, it's me."

"Where the hell are you?" he snapped when he heard her voice. "Everyone's looking for you. Is Shep with you, dammit? Are you hurt?"

She filled him in, in as few words as possible, and gave her location, requested backup, then hung up. The team would have to negotiate their next step with the Mexican government, but that was their task now. She had plenty of items on her own to-do list, the two at the top being keeping Yo Tee secured until the team got here and stopping his men from killing Shep downstairs.

She handed the phone to Yo Tee. "Call your men and tell them to bring my partner up here."

He didn't move.

"Fine, then we'll go to him." All she wanted was to hole up in some defensible position with Shep and Yo Tee until the team arrived.

"Where are the people you're planning on smuggling across the border?" she asked as she considered her options.

"I don't know what you talking about. All I know is U.S. government agent broke into my place of business held me at gunpoint. Neither of my governments be happy about that. I'm Chinese-Mexican and respected businessman in both countries."

"That'll end soon," she promised. "Where are the terrorists? Are they here? In this building?"

His lips narrowed; hate flared in his gaze.

She couldn't have cared less about his feelings. "Have they already left for Galmer's Gulley?"

He couldn't keep the surprise from his face when she mentioned the location, confirming the intel Shep's team had gathered. Good to know they were on the right track.

"I don't know what you talking about," he told her.

"Where are the chemical weapons?"

"We make paper here," he said, as cocky and superior as could be. "You crazy woman."

She wanted to shoot him.

She'd shot people before, but never without reluctance, never unless it was the last resort, in an effort to stop them from harming others. This was honestly the first time she wanted to put a bullet through an unarmed man's kneecap.

Short of doing violence, she didn't think she was going to get him to talk, and maybe not even then. But Shep's team could handle that, she decided, when they got here. This wasn't the right time and place for an interrogation anyway, not when his men could burst through the door any second.

She scanned the room, then scanned Yo Tee. "Take off your belt."

"You want my pants off." He sounded amused now. "That against some American law. You so very politically correct all the time."

"Your belt. Now."

He shrugged and took off the belt then tossed it to her.

She walked around him, keeping the gun aimed at his head. "Hands behind your back."

He complied after a moment of hesitation. "My men kill you as soon we leave this room. You know. Why not talk reasonable?"

She bound his wrists together with the belt, kept the long end to hold him like a dog on a leash. "You'll walk in front of me. Out. Now. Move."

He did, walking to the door leisurely, then out into the entryway. He looked at the dead man lying on the floor and kicked him in the head as they walked by him, apparently dissatisfied with his service.

The hallway still stood empty. Good. She moved forward. "To the staircase."

"Your people can't come here without authorization from my government. Diplomacy takes long time. Days. You think you hold an entire factory with single gun that long?"

"I'm not the type to give up."

He took his time walking down the hallway, but they reached the stairs at last and started down. "Bravery a noble thing. Courage my people much appreciate. But a difference between bravery and stupidity."

She held the gun on him. "Let that be my worry."

"You and your friend get free leave, a car and

suitcase full of money. You go wherever you want. You never have to go back across border again. You live happy long life down south on nice beach. Better than dying today, eh?"

"I'm not planning on dying."

But just as she said that, half a dozen armed men poured out into the staircase down below. From the way they all swung their rifles around to aim at her, it looked as if she might not get a choice in the matter.

She couldn't get to Shep this way. She couldn't get anywhere if she was shot. So she yanked Yo Tee back. "Come on!"

She ran back toward his office with him while the men rushed up the stairs behind them, shouting. She fixed her gaze on the office at the end of the hallway and did her level best to reach it, even with Yo Tee resisting. The steel security door would offer more protection against siege than anything else she'd seen so far in the building.

She had about a minute to reach it.

Chapter Twelve

Shep lay on the floor, all bloodied, waiting for them to be done with him, focused on protecting his body rather than trying to fight his way through a wall of armed men. Six, he could have handled. Twelve, he couldn't. And he was determined to stay alive so he could help Lilly escape from here. So for the moment, instead of fighting, he did his best to appear limp and lifeless.

They weren't here to kill him; they were just taking their anger out on him. At some point, they'd be finished.

The tactic worked. When shouting rose from somewhere deep inside the building, most of the men ran to whatever new alarm had been raised.

Only two remained, each holding their rifles on him.

He kept his eyes open only a slit, playing the part of a mortally injured man to the hilt. Not that difficult when he was in a world of hurt. He gave a weak groan and shifted, the move taking him maybe a foot closer to the bastards.

Then he drew a slow breath, filling up his lungs. And then the next second his right hand snaked out, grabbed the nearest rifle barrel even as he vaulted to his feet and shoved the man into his buddy, twisting the rifle away from him in the same movement.

The men were on the floor and Shep on them now, with ruthless efficiency. He didn't want gunshots, didn't want the others to come rushing back, so he bashed in the armed man's head first, then his buddy's as the bastard tried to roll away from him. They stayed down, the both of them.

Shep pushed to his feet, grabbed both rifles then ran through the door and followed the sounds of angry shouting all the way to a staircase. On the floor above him, he could hear men rushing up the stairs. He had a fair idea why. Since Lilly had gone to the roof and was probably on one of the top floors, it was fair to assume that she'd been spotted.

He kept close to the wall and ran up after the men. None of them were looking back down. They were all focused on something above them, pushing each other out of the way to reach the top faster. Shep pushed as hard as he could, trying to catch up without being noticed.

Gunshots were ringing out by the time he reached the first floor. He was the only person in the staircase now; the others had gotten up all the way and pushed out of sight on the third floor, the gun battle intensifying.

He ran up silently, as fast as he could, a rifle in one hand, the other slung across his shoulder. He needed to reach Lilly before it was too late.

He didn't care if she was here to assess his team. He just wanted her to stay alive.

He loved her. It became crystal clear the moment she'd disappeared through the window. He'd somehow, in the space of three days, fallen in love with Lilly. Whether or not they could ever have anything serious between them was the question.

He pushed the thought away. *Not now.*

But soon. Whatever her true purpose was for being with his team, they'd have to talk about it and sort all that out. But it wasn't going to change how he felt about her. He ran forward to save her.

He only slowed when he reached the top floor and spotted twenty or so armed men crowded at the far end in front of a steel security door, banging with their rifles, trying to break it down. They weren't making much progress. The door looked pretty heavy-duty.

He had a feeling Lilly was behind it. Smart woman. One of the reasons he'd fallen for her.

He squeezed off a round of shots at the men, then ducked behind cover as they shot back.

He didn't know how many he'd hit, but he knew that whoever was left uninjured would be coming for him. He swung both his rifles over his shoulder, ran back down the stairs and jumped through the first open door he saw on the second floor, locked the door behind him, ran to the window. Then out he went without hesitation, wanting to be out of sight by the time they broke the door down.

He needed to go up, to Lilly, but the window directly above him was closed. Smashing it in would have given away his location, so he looked to the next one, just a few feet over. The glass pane stood open a crack.

He maneuvered that way, his cowboy boots not exactly meant for climbing like this, slipping more than once. He hung on with everything he had. Failure was not an option.

When he reached the windowsill, he grabbed on tight and pulled himself up to look in. Another empty office. Maybe Yo Tee had the factory on shutdown for today, to get ready for the transfer.

He hung on with his right hand while opening the window wider with the left. *Okay. Deep breath. Focus.* Now would not be a good time to slip.

He didn't. He pulled himself up and in.

This office was a mess, chairs turned over, the drawers on the filing cabinet hanging open. Bullet holes dotted the walls. Looked as if Yo Tee might have had a disagreement with one of his managers.

Disagreement in the ranks was rarely good for business. Or for your health, if your boss was the Coyote.

Shep moved to the door and could hear people talking at the far end of the hallway. Some of the men had run off to chase him, but others had remained at that steel door, still trying to figure out how to get in. And they'd be watching their backs this time; he wasn't going to be able to take them by surprise again.

His next move was a risky one, but he had to make it anyway.

He filled his lungs and burst out into the hall, firing at them as he went. Six men shot back at him, barricaded behind four bodies, those he'd taken out earlier.

He shot down one more before he had to pull back in.

He glanced at his left arm where a bullet had ripped through his skin. Nothing serious. The injury was nearly identical to Lilly's. They'd have matching scars to commemorate their mis-adventures. Provided they lived.

Five men remained at the end of the hallway, and the other ten or so who'd run downstairs to find him would be coming back now that they'd heard the gunshots. They were likely to figure out that he'd outsmarted them and doubled back somehow.

The small office he occupied was not a good defensible position, the door made of inch-wide simple wood, nothing to hide behind that would stop bullets. So out the window he went again.

Man, he hated this part.

He didn't have any phobias, but he wasn't a fan of heights. He went on regardless. The first thing he'd learned in this job was that as soon as a person let fear stop them, they were dead.

He didn't try to get into the next room or the one after that. He climbed handhold by handhold all the way to the end so he'd be outside the room with the steel door at the end of the hallway.

He looked in carefully, not wanting to get his head blown off in case Lilly took him for one of Yo Tee's men.

She was in there, armed to the teeth, crouching behind a makeshift barricade of desks and chairs, facing the door. Yo Tee sat tied to a chair with his own belt in the corner.

When Shep rapped on the glass, she swung around, her rifle aimed. Her eyes went wide when she recognized him.

"Let me in."

She hurried over. "You okay?" She looked at the blood on his arm as she opened the window.

"It's nothing. You?"

"We're trapped. But at least I called reinforcements."

Of course she did. While evading a band of armed killers and capturing one of the biggest crime bosses south of the border. She was nothing if not efficient. He grinned at her. "I decided to forgive you if you promise to get out of this mess alive."

She raised a questioning eyebrow. And when he said nothing more, she nodded. "Okay. Fine."

Being in the same room with her made him feel a hell of a lot better, but they weren't out of the woods yet. "There's a pretty big group of armed thugs in front of the door."

"How many?"

"Fifteen or so. There were about two dozen. I took a few out." He glanced at Yo Tee. "I think he shut down operations and has just enough security here with him to set up the transfer."

She shot a dark glare at the Coyote.

He knew what she was thinking. They were

both well armed. Between the two of them, they could probably break out of here and get to a truck. But they couldn't risk Yo Tee getting killed. The bastard had to stay alive long enough to be interrogated.

Gunfire sounded outside.

She shot him a questioning look.

He shook his head. "Can't be the reinforcements yet." Not enough time had passed for that.

More gunfire came. And this time it was clear that the steel door was getting hit. Yo Tee's men had decided to shoot the door down to rescue him.

Shep glanced back the way he'd come, at the window.

She followed his gaze. "Can't go that way."

She was right. They couldn't go through the window, not with Yo Tee resisting.

But the door wouldn't hold long. The men outside were firing round after round into the lock. While it was a reinforced steel door, it wasn't strong enough to stand up to this kind of siege.

Shep grabbed Yo Tee, chair and all, and dragged him to the corner to the left of the door, where at least the first volley of bullets to come through couldn't hit him. He pulled a bookshelf away from the wall a little so the man wouldn't be immediately visible when his lackeys broke in.

He gagged the man just as the door gave a mighty crack.

"Get in the other corner," he ordered Lilly, a plan forming in his head.

Lilly did as he asked, wedging into the office's corner behind the door, where she wouldn't be seen when the outer steel door finally broke down.

Shep lay down in the middle of the room, pulling Lilly's makeshift barricade on top of him until he was buried under furniture. He hoped that, at least at first glance, the room would look deserted as the men pushed their way in. A moment of confusion, a second of pause was all he needed.

The steel door shook. They were ramming it, probably lined up shoulder to shoulder, hoping to snap the damaged lock. Still, the steel didn't give.

But the brick wall did, cracking and crumbling, releasing the lock.

The door banged open. The shouting stopped then restarted again as the men ran across the empty outer room into the office, jumping over the knocked-down pile of furniture on their way to the open window.

"Where are they?" more than one shouted in Spanish.

"They went down. Outside," one of the men shouted.

They'd see Yo Tee in a second, as soon as they turned. So Shep rose, kicking furniture off him, aiming at the men who had nowhere to run, no place to hide.

Lilly sprung from behind the door, slamming the wood into the faces of a handful of stragglers, knocking them back. She opened fire as the door swung open again, backing toward Shep until they were shoulder to shoulder. Neither of them removed their fingers from the trigger until there were no more enemies standing.

They were both breathing hard, both bleeding and injured when the gun smoke settled, but alive—a miracle. The carnage in the room was incredible, the bloodiest destruction that could be achieved in just a few minutes.

Yo Tee was on the ground, on his side. He'd pushed his chair over to keep down. He was staring at them wide-eyed as if they were crazy people.

Lilly went to straighten him. She pulled the gag from his mouth.

"Work for me," he said in a shaky voice. "I make you both millionaires."

"No thanks," Lilly told him.

Shep moved to make sure all the men were down for good. He didn't want to be surprised by a bullet to his back.

Satisfied that none of the men would pop up for a surprise attack, Shep moved closer to Lilly to look her over. Her clothes were ripped and she had some scrapes plus a serious flesh wound, but it didn't look as if any vital organs had been hit. She was standing up, not holding any body parts, a good sign.

"Hey." She was scanning him for injury in return. "You know where to buy a lottery ticket around here? I'm thinking this is our lucky day."

He grinned at her. He wanted to take her into his arms more than anything. But they weren't done yet.

He walked up to Yo Tee and rested the barrel of his rifle against the man's forehead. "Where are the men that you're sending over the border?"

Lilly moved to the door to watch for any possible newcomers. She had her weapon ready to greet anyone who might be ill-advised enough to come after the others.

"I don't know what you talking about," Yo Tee said, his dark eyes filled with hate.

Shep held his gaze. "If the last few minutes taught you anything, it should be that I don't play nice." He wiped his hand on his pants, leaving a crimson stain, then shrugged. "Blood never really bothered me."

Yo Tee looked away first.

"Are they coming here to be put in the back of trucks tonight?"

They could be arriving even now, in which case a reception committee would have to be set up for them. Although, if Shep's luck held, they wouldn't come until after his team had gotten here.

"There's no easy way out of this now," he warned Yo Tee. "There's only the hard way and the harder way. Trust me, if there's anything you can tell me now, it'll save you considerable grief when the rest of my team gets here. They're even worse at playing nice than I am." He paused, then he moved close enough to crowd the man. "When are your buddies arriving here?"

Yo Tee gave a superior smile. "They come and gone. You too late."

He looked cocky and pleased with himself enough to make Shep think he might not be lying.

"When?"

"The first day news came about extra attention on the border. As soon as patrols stepped up and crackdowns on smuggling started." He looked damn proud of himself, sticking his chest out. "My men got them across without trouble. They been in U.S. for weeks."

Shep grabbed him by the front of his shirt and pulled him half off the chair. "Where are they now?"

The man stared into his eyes without flinching. "They paid me. They didn't share plans with me."

Shep watched him, inclined to believe the words, yet something about the man's body language was off, something in the way his eyes darted.

He lowered his gun as he turned back to Lilly. "Better call off reinforcements. No sense in more people coming. It'd be better if we grabbed a truck and drove back across the border on our own. Nobody would even know that we've been here. Might as well avoid an international incident if we can."

Maybe she picked up on the game he was playing, because she nodded toward Yo Tee. "What about him?"

"He has no more useful information. If his body is found with his men, local police will write it off as a battle between rival drug bosses. No sense dragging the U.S. into this."

"No! I have money—" Yo Tee protested.

Chapter Thirteen

Lilly watched as Shep shrugged at the offer of riches.

"I don't care about money. I'm here for information," he said. "You have to know more." He didn't look as if he was buying the man's I-know-nothing act.

Lilly wasn't, either. If the terrorists had crossed the border weeks ago, why the smuggling moratorium that had been strictly enforced by Yo Tee's men? That had to have cost millions, to him and his smuggling buddies. He wouldn't have done that without good reason.

She glanced down the hallway—still empty—then back to him. "So what's planned for tonight at Galmer's Gulley?"

The man pressed his narrow lips together so tightly they nearly disappeared.

Shep put the rifle barrel right between his eyes. "What are you sending across the border tonight?"

She knew him, she was in love with him, and the way he growled at the man still sent a shiver of apprehension down her spine.

Tension and the sense of impending violence filled the air, the silence broken by a single word Yo Tee squeaked out at last. "Weapons."

Lilly glanced at the hallway. He might still have men in the building, recouping and planning another attack. But there was nobody in sight, so she looked at Yo Tee again, waiting for more. According to confirmed intel, those terrorists were going to bring chemical weapons into the U.S.

Shep glared at his captive. "Why didn't the weapons go with the men?"

"The vials weren't ready yet." Yo Tee hesitated. "They wanted a lot, and the lab messed up first batch."

"Where are the vials?"

But that was the question Yo Tee decided to make his last stand on, because he just stared straight ahead and wouldn't say a single word no matter what Shep threatened him with next.

THE MEXICAN AUTHORITIES arrived first, but they didn't enter. They simply secured the perimeter and locked down the entire factory compound, as far as Shep could tell from the window. They probably had their orders. Looked as if some kind of international deal had been made at the last second.

It wasn't long after that his team arrived on FBI choppers. Shep debriefed them and passed on the latest intel about the terrorists to the Colonel via a secure phone. Yo Tee was immediately flown out to a secure location by the FBI for further interrogation, while Shep's team searched the building for the chemical weapons.

Unfortunately, several hours of thorough work later, they still didn't have anything. Tension mounted higher and higher as they went over ground they'd already covered. By the time Shep ran into Lilly at the loading docks, he was brimming with frustration.

She was eyeing the truck they'd passed while being marched inside when they'd first arrived, five giant rolls of paper in the back, one still on the loading dock.

She narrowed her eyes as she measured up the roll. "We know the weapons were about to be shipped to the border. This would make sense."

"They've been scanned. No traces of chemical agents," he told her. "We haven't found any traces in the whole damn factory."

But she kept looking. "Because the lab isn't here. If the vials came here in airtight containers, all they would have received here would have been extra wrapping. No contamination."

Shep pulled out his cell and called Ryder. "Do we have a plain old metal detector?"

"If we don't, we can get one. Where do you need it?"

"Loading docks." He walked around the roll still waiting to be loaded. Nothing looked disturbed, nothing betrayed that anyone had messed with the paper, no cuts, no bulges.

Lilly strode over. "Boost me up."

He did, and she moved without hesitation. They had practice at this.

She banged on the top of the giant roll, felt around. "Doesn't look like anything has been inserted through here. Maybe through the bottom." She jumped down.

Shep gave the roll a push, but it didn't budge an inch. It had to weigh a ton. "Let's try that with a forklift." There were plenty of those around.

He hopped on one and drove it over, tipped the giant roll to its side, then got out to inspect the bottom. He crouched next to Lilly, the both of them running their fingers over the ridged surface of layers and layers of paper, looking for any hidden openings.

By the time they were done, finding nothing, a Mexican army Jeep was driving up. The arriving lieutenant handed Shep a metal detector without asking any questions, then drove away.

"The collaboration is going better than expected," Lilly remarked.

Shep turned on the professional-grade instrument. "I bet it's the Colonel's doing." If there was anything the Colonel, the head of the SDDU, couldn't do, Shep hadn't seen it yet. The man was a legend in the unit.

He started scanning the roll of paper on the bottom and moved up, careful not to miss an inch. He was at the midpoint when the metal detector went off, issuing a series of loud beeps.

He put the detector down and pulled out his cell phone, called Ryder. "I think we have something."

"We'll be there in a minute."

Lilly tapped the roll as he was hanging up. "Looks like the paper was wrapped around the container in the middle. I don't think unrolling it here would be wise."

He agreed. "We'll transport everything back to the U.S."

"How about I take care of that?" She reached out a hand for the cell phone. "I'll request a reinforced truck that's built for this kind of thing. Bombproof and airtight. They'll take everything to a special lab in D.C. for containment and analysis."

Ryder was running from the back, overhearing that last bit. "That sounds like the best plan of action. How fast can they get here?"

"Couple of hours."

Shep handed her the cell phone, and she dialed while he shot Ryder a questioning look. It wasn't like their team leader to let the bureau swoop in and take over without a fight.

"We have terrorists to catch on the border." He scanned the roll of paper. "In there?"

Shep nodded. "Looks like it."

Ryder grabbed the metal detector and checked again, then jumped up to the back of the truck and scanned the rest of the rolls. Every single one of them beeped.

The rest of the team was coming from the factory by the time he came back out.

Jamie spoke first. "What do we have here?"

"Probably enough chemical weapons to take out Capitol Hill," Shep told him. "The FBI will transport them to their lab safely. We'll take the truck to our meeting with the tangos." So they wouldn't suspect that anything had gone wrong. The van had plenty of room in the back for a couple of surprises—his whole team and some serious weaponry.

Ryder gestured toward Jamie with his head. "You'll drive the truck back. The rest of us will wait here for the FBI then catch up to you with the choppers."

Jamie nodded and moved toward the forklift. "Let's get these rolls unloaded."

While he did that, Shep took the metal detector and scanned all the rolls remaining on the loading dock to make sure they hadn't missed anything. But the metal detector didn't go off again.

Jamie left with the truck, and the rest of the team went back inside the factory to finish their search of the floor and offices, hoping to find some information on the terrorists. They didn't. So they looked again. And again.

He went to the basement with Lilly.

She stopped as they reached the bottom of the stairs. "Thanks for having my back today. I mean it." She smiled. "There's something I've been thinking about. We're good together and I'm in—"

"You're in a difficult position. I know. You're supposed to evaluate us and we had this... thing," he said rapidly, afraid that she might go in another direction.

She could have been killed today. He couldn't handle the thought. He could have been killed, too. They'd make a terrible couple. Neither of them would have a worry-free moment. This was not the life he wanted for her.

"Anyway. You do the job you were sent here to do. We made a mistake. We won't make it again. It's no big deal. Just forget it, all right?"

The smile slid off her face. A stricken look came into her eyes, but she blinked it away as she turned from him, her shoulders stiff. "Forgotten already. I'll go left." She started out with hurried strides. "You go right. Call out if you find anything."

But neither of them did.

Hours passed before the FBI's special truck arrived.

Ryder let them take over at that point and ordered his team onto the choppers.

Shep ran with the others, glanced back, slowed when he saw Lilly still standing by the FBI truck, talking with the agents who'd come with it. He waited for her to turn. He wanted at least to give her a last wave.

But she didn't look his way.

"Shep?" Ryder called for him.

"Coming." He didn't know what he would say to her, even if he could run back. And he couldn't. They both had jobs to do.

He ducked his head to avoid the spinning rotors and pulled himself into the chopper, hung on as the bird lifted and banked sharply to the left.

He watched as she finally lifted her head, pausing in the conversation to look after him.

Her job with his team was done. She'd be

going straight to D.C. with the truck. He wasn't going to see her again, which was for the best.

But the thought squeezed his heart, sending a pang of pain deep into his chest.

NIGHT HAD FALLEN and the borderlands were deserted, the Rio Grande a dark ribbon, snaking in the distance. Keith drove the paper-factory truck, Shep and Jamie in the back. The other three men on the team had taken the three best strategic high points around Galmer's Gulley.

When the SDDU's Texas headquarters had first been established, a dozen men had been assigned to the task. Six came to their trailer office, and another six had been sent to South America to trace why and from where the terrorists were coming.

They weren't Middle Eastern as first assumed. They were part of the South American drug cartels. They'd come in response to the U.S. shift in drug control toward stricter measures. The cartels had bought many politicians in their own countries. Those who couldn't be bought they killed. And now they decided to put U.S. lawmakers in their crosshairs, apparently.

Most likely, the attack was to be the first in a campaign of intimidation. The threat had to be tracked to the source. Except everything had turned out to be more complicated and dangerous than anticipated, so the rest of the team was still stuck in South America.

The Texas half had to handle tonight on their own. And they would, if Shep had anything to do with it. They'd been here way too long, preparing for this moment.

Small holes had been drilled into the side of the truck and in the doors in the back so he and Jamie could see out. The team members were all in radio contact with each other.

Keith drove to the exact coordinates Yo Tee had finally given up to the FBI just half an hour ago. Nothing like leaving things to the last possible moment.

Keith pulled the truck into a spot where the elevation and some mesquite would keep it out of sight as much as possible. Someone who smuggled the kind of load he was supposed to be carrying wouldn't stay out in the open advertising it to every border agent who happened by.

Then they waited.

And waited.

Long minutes ticked by before Mo said, "Movement at the north end of the gulley," over the radio. "I see two."

"Two more a little lower," Ryder added.

"Another two on my side." That came from Ray.

Okay, all six were here now. Yo Tee had confessed to transporting six, more than the original intel had indicated, but the team could definitely handle this many.

But then Mo said, "Wait. I got more movement. Two more. I have four here altogether."

And as Shep watched the moonlit landscape, he noticed more movement. "And four more coming in the back way."

Either Yo Tee had lied or the terrorists had come in two groups and never told him about the second just to be on the safe side.

Jamie swore quietly next to him.

"Twelve. Everybody got that? Anybody seeing more?" Ryder was asking, but nobody responded. "We have a full dozen, then," he finished after a minute.

They were outnumbered two to one.

"What kind of weapons?" Shep asked. The men he was watching approached on foot and kept to the shadows and indentations of the land, making it difficult to see what they were carrying.

"Semiautomatics," Keith said from up front. Apparently, he had a better angle.

"Ah, hell," Ray swore. "One of mine has a grenade launcher. He's staying behind while the others are moving forward."

"Must be their plan B," Jamie said next to Shep. Shep gripped his weapon tighter. A grenade launcher could take out the truck and everyone in it. Their bulletproof vests wouldn't be able to help a damn.

"Coming my way," Ray whispered.

Made sense. The guy with the grenade launcher would want the high point, too.

"Take him out quietly," Ryder ordered.

"I can see five now on my side," Shep told Jamie.

"I see three on mine. They all stopped."

"Do I get out?" Keith asked.

"Stay in the cab," Ryder told him. "Let them initiate."

The men started walking again. Three went up to the cab, five to the back. The one with the grenade launcher was climbing to Ray's high point, so that left three more out there somewhere, watching from out of sight.

Shep could hear the truck's door open, Keith's boots slapping to the ground as he got out.

He greeted them in Spanish. "Everything's okay. You take this truck, I have a ride waiting to take me back across the border." His grandfather had been Mexican. He had enough of the blood in him to pass for a Mexican driver, especially in the dark.

"Open the back first. Let's see." One of the men barked the words at him.

Shep and Jamie braced themselves for action.

They had a Kevlar shield set up in front of them to duck behind, stretching the width of the truck and three feet high. As they held their weapons ready, sounds of a scuffle came over the radio.

Then Ray said, "Got him."

Okay. The grenade launcher was out of the equation.

And not a minute too soon, since the next second the lock turned and the double back doors of the van swung open to the night.

Keith was smart enough to lunge to the left, tuck and roll and disappear behind the cover of some rocks as everyone opened fire and all hell broke loose.

A bullet grazed Shep's ear. He ducked behind the barricade then up again to squeeze off another round of shots.

Two men fell. Jamie was knocked back when a bullet hit his shoulder.

Shep charged forward, vaulting over the barricade to take the heat off him.

Keith stopped shooting from the side to avoid accidentally hitting his teammates.

Three of the enemy were still standing, the rest badly injured or dead. Shep shot another one as he landed, then pivoted to the left to shoot after one who'd decided to flee.

He caught sight of Keith on the ground, holding both hands over his neck, blood gushing through his fingers.

Shep rushed toward him, firing into the night, providing him with cover. There were plenty of shots coming out of the darkness. He felt a bullet rip into his thigh just as he reached Keith, jarring him, knocking him sideways. He flattened himself to the ground next to Keith.

Then Jamie was there, laying down cover.

More shots in the distance. Probably Mo and Ray coming in. There couldn't have been more than a man or two left of the tangos, but the gunfight still went on.

Shep saw movement behind some brush, caught a glimpse of a face he didn't recognize. He shot the bastard without thinking.

And that was the last one. No more bullets came after that.

"You always want them all to yourself. One of these days you're going to have to learn how to share," Jamie groused next to him.

"Watch for more." He bit out the words as he kneeled next to Keith and grabbed his radio unit. "Man down. We need a chopper ASAP."

"Who is it?" Ryder asked.

"Keith. What's going on at your end?"

"I got one. Running up. I'll be there in a minute."

"Got two," Mo said. "How bad is Keith?"

"Pretty bad."

"Sounds like we have our twelve," Jamie remarked, but kept alert, still scanning their surroundings.

Chapter Fourteen

Lilly sat alone in her home office in D.C. as she finished her report and saved it on her laptop. She'd made her official recommendation. The SDDU's Texas team had to stay where they were. She made it clear that in her opinion, their presence was a matter of national security.

The op had been a complete success, and all the loose ends had been tied up in the two weeks since. The chemical weapons had been destroyed, the surviving terrorists interrogated.

She hadn't gone back to Pebble Creek. She had the hotel mail her things to D.C. She figured she'd caused enough grief in Shep's life already. He'd made it clear that he didn't want anything to do with her. He didn't need her hanging around with her confused and conflicted feelings. So she'd given him a clean break.

But when her phone rang, just as she shut her computer down, and his name came up on the display screen, her heart thrilled.

"I'd like to take you to dinner," he said without preamble.

His voice filled her with longing, but she tried to keep things light. "Next time I'm in town?"

"Actually, I'm in D.C. I could pick you up tonight. Or when you're free."

"Tonight is good," she said, suddenly breathless.

"Address?"

She smiled at that. "You didn't run a full background check on me? I'd have thought you would have all my personal details." His team had access to databases that were better than the FBI's.

"That would have been stalking. This is…"

Part of her hoped he would finish with *a date*.

But he said something so much better. "This is a man asking the woman he loves to have dinner with him."

Now, could anyone have said no to that? Not likely. Her heart was melting on the spot. Yet she wasn't sure what to stay in response, the words stuck inside her chest. At the end, she simply gave him her address.

"When can I pick you up?"

She ran her fingers through her hair. "Half an hour?" Best if she didn't have too much time to obsess.

"I'll be there."

She showered and dressed, brushed some makeup on with nervous fingers. She'd barely finished with her hair when the doorbell rang.

She lived in a secure condo building, so she pushed the button to let him in downstairs, then waited for him at her door.

"Hey." His voice was even better in person than over the phone.

God, she'd missed him. For the longest time, all she wanted was to be an independent woman. She wanted to be someone who could take care of herself, someone who didn't need anyone. It was a hell of a thing to realize now that she needed Shep.

She swallowed. "Hey."

He pulled a bouquet of lilies from behind his back with the hottest smile she'd ever seen.

Lilies were her favorite, her namesake flower. When she was a little girl, being named after a flower made her feel special. She liked to be associated with something beautiful when her life was anything but. She'd told him that once, long ago.

"Thank you." She took the flowers. "I can't believe you remembered."

She moved back, which turned out to be a mistake. If she'd moved forward instead, out into the hallway, ready to go, they might have made it to the restaurant.

As it was, Shep followed her in.

She pulled a vase from under the sink, filled it with water and set the flowers in it, then placed them on the kitchen table. "How's the team?"

"Good. Keith will be reinstated to full duty next week. Brian and Tank are in jail." He stood in the middle of her living room, watching her. "Nice place," he said without really looking around. He kept his eyes on her.

"I spend most of my time at work. I'm barely here," she said inanely, when all she wanted to do was scream *You said you loved me!*

"Working on anything exciting?"

Good grief, if the tension was any thicker in the room, it would have been visible.

"Can't really talk about that." She took a step toward him, but then stopped. Maybe she'd misunderstood him on the phone. Maybe she heard what she wanted to hear. "You?"

"The same." He stepped toward her and held her gaze. "I missed you. I want us to be together."

Her heart banged so hard against her rib cage she thought she was going to pass out.

"We'd make a terrible couple. We couldn't talk about anything." Stuff was just coming out of her mouth and she couldn't stop it. "Everything we do is confidential."

"We'll find something else to fill our time with."

"Why did you change your mind?"

"I went to the hospital with Keith when they took him in. A bullet just about ripped his throat out. We didn't think he was going to make it. The only thing he said was he wished he asked you out while he had the chance."

She watched him, not entirely understanding his point.

He reached out, took her hand and pulled her slowly against him. "All I could think was that if I was lying there on my deathbed, that would be my biggest regret, too. Letting you go."

He gave her time to pull away, but she had no intention of protesting. When he lowered his lips to hers, relief flooded her. At least if he kissed her, she wouldn't be able to say anything else stupid.

Nothing in this world felt half as good as being held in Shep's arms and being kissed by him.

But too soon, he pulled away. "So how is this going to work?"

"Tonight?" she asked, dazed.

He gave a wicked grin. "I'm pretty sure I can figure tonight out."

Her core temperature shot up a few degrees.

He rested his forehead against hers. "I meant the future. Together."

Right. With her in D.C. and him in Texas. "We could meet in the middle. Spend the weekends together."

"Not enough," he protested immediately. "I could leave the team."

She pulled back to stare at him. "You would?" That was mind-boggling. She considered it for a long second before she shook her head. "You already lost a job because of me. This one is right for you. It matters." She paused. "I could come to Texas."

He watched her carefully. "You're building a career here."

"Career isn't everything. There's something else I always wanted to do." She paused for a second. "I told you I've been thinking about working with kids in the system. Kids in foster care who get in trouble with the law. I'd love to put together some kind of program to turn them in another direction. If I could get government funding…"

A smile spread on his face. "You'd be perfect for the job."

His vote of confidence felt good. "I hope so. I really think there's a need." She paused. "I always thought I might be good with something like that. While I might not be good at, you know, kids in a family setting."

There. One of her deepest secrets. She'd never seen how mothering worked, not up close and personal. She didn't have those experiences. She hadn't planned on giving that a try, didn't want to mess up some poor little kid.

"I don't agree, but we'll cross that bridge when we get to it." He kissed her again. "I do like your idea of helping foster kids, though. You could start in Texas, maybe even build something that goes nationwide. You have government contacts. I have a few of my own. If we have downtime, the team and I could offer some boot-camp training. Grace Cordero, Ryder's girlfriend, is looking for ways to use her ranch. She had corporate boot camps there before. And she has animals there, too. Juvenile rehab with kids working with rescue animals is a big thing—"

She put a finger over his lips, enormously gratified how excited he was about her idea, how supportive. But for now... "We'll brainstorm in the morning. For now I just want you to kiss me."

Normally, he didn't take orders well, but at the moment he looked happy to obey.

He kissed her and then some, making her head spin. But just as she was about to drown in his touch, his familiar, masculine scent, in the feel of his mouth over hers, he pulled back again, with a pained expression on his face.

"What is it?"

He blew some air from his lungs. "Since the first time...I practically attacked you. We just fell in bed and...I wanted this to be sweet and long and more romantic. I don't want to rush it."

"You want to go to dinner?"

"No," he admitted.

"Me, neither."

His face lit up.

"You're a commando. I'm an FBI agent. We don't do slow," she reminded him. "I want fast."

"You don't always get what you want in a relationship. There's the whole compromise thing." He lifted her and walked toward the bedroom.

"How is this a compromise?"

"I wanted to take you on the carpet."

HIS BODY WAS READY, poised at her opening as she straddled him on the bed.

"I love you, too," she said.

His heart was about to burst.

She smiled. "I think we should get our own ranch."

Okay. He inched his fingers up her naked thigh.

"And I want horses. If we live in Texas, you're going to have to learn how to ride well."

She was going to discuss livestock?

He grabbed her hips and pulled her down on him, sheathed himself in her wet heat to the hilt. His eyes rolled back in his head from the pleasure.

Her breath caught and she gave a quick little moan that nearly sent him over the edge.

But then she seemed to recover. "And I think we should—"

"All right, that's it." He flipped her in a lightning-quick move so she was sprawled under him the next second.

Her eyes widened. "You're still very bossy. I have to say, you didn't mellow much with age."

He raised an eyebrow as he withdrew and then pushed in again. "You want me mellow?"

She arched her back. "On second thought, not really."

"We're doing this all the way. I want it all. There'll be no casual dating, no seeing other people. When I commit to something, it's 100 percent."

She ran her slim fingers up his chest and brushed the pads over his nipples. "I like that about you."

His entire body tightened. "Then you won't object to marrying me right away?"

"For Mitch's sake?"

"Because I love you so much I can't see straight."

"What if I wreck your life again?"

He looked deep into her eyes. "I'm pretty sure you're going to make it." He dipped his head for a kiss as he made her his.

* * * * *

LARGER-PRINT BOOKS!
GET 2 FREE LARGER-PRINT NOVELS PLUS
2 FREE GIFTS!

◊ HARLEQUIN®

INTRIGUE®

BREATHTAKING ROMANTIC SUSPENSE

YES! Please send me 2 FREE LARGER-PRINT Harlequin Intrigue® novels and my 2 FREE gifts (gifts are worth about $10). After receiving them, if I don't wish to receive any more books, I can return the shipping statement marked "cancel." If I don't cancel, I will receive 6 brand-new novels every month and be billed just $5.49 per book in the U.S. or $5.99 per book in Canada. That's a saving of at least 13% off the cover price! It's quite a bargain! Shipping and handling is just 50¢ per book in the U.S. and 75¢ per book in Canada.* I understand that accepting the 2 free books and gifts places me under no obligation to buy anything. I can always return a shipment and cancel at any time. Even if I never buy another book, the two free books and gifts are mine to keep forever.

199/399 HDN F42Y

Name	(PLEASE PRINT)	
Address		Apt. #
City	State/Prov.	Zip/Postal Code

Signature (if under 18, a parent or guardian must sign)

Mail to the **Harlequin® Reader Service:**
IN U.S.A.: P.O. Box 1867, Buffalo, NY 14240-1867
IN CANADA: P.O. Box 609, Fort Erie, Ontario L2A 5X3

**Are you a subscriber to Harlequin Intrigue books
and want to receive the larger-print edition?
Call 1-800-873-8635 today or visit www.ReaderService.com.**

* Terms and prices subject to change without notice. Prices do not include applicable taxes. Sales tax applicable in N.Y. Canadian residents will be charged applicable taxes. Offer not valid in Quebec. This offer is limited to one order per household. Not valid for current subscribers to Harlequin Intrigue Larger-Print books. All orders subject to credit approval. Credit or debit balances in a customer's account(s) may be offset by any other outstanding balance owed by or to the customer. Please allow 4 to 6 weeks for delivery. Offer available while quantities last.

Your Privacy—The Harlequin® Reader Service is committed to protecting your privacy. Our Privacy Policy is available online at www.ReaderService.com or upon request from the Harlequin Reader Service.

We make a portion of our mailing list available to reputable third parties that offer products we believe may interest you. If you prefer that we not exchange your name with third parties, or if you wish to clarify or modify your communication preferences, please visit us at www.ReaderService.com/consumerchoice or write to us at Harlequin Reader Service Preference Service, P.O. Box 9062, Buffalo, NY 14269. Include your complete name and address.

HILP13R

LARGER-PRINT BOOKS!

GET 2 FREE LARGER-PRINT NOVELS PLUS 2 FREE MYSTERY GIFTS

Love Inspired®

SUSPENSE
RIVETING INSPIRATIONAL ROMANCE

Larger-print novels are now available...

YES! Please send me 2 FREE LARGER-PRINT Love Inspired® Suspense novels and my 2 FREE mystery gifts (gifts are worth about $10). After receiving them, if I don't wish to receive any more books, I can return the shipping statement marked "cancel." If I don't cancel, I will receive 4 brand-new novels every month and be billed just $5.24 per book in the U.S. or $5.74 per book in Canada. That's a savings of at least 23% off the cover price. It's quite a bargain! Shipping and handling is just 50¢ per book in the U.S. and 75¢ per book in Canada.* I understand that accepting the 2 free books and gifts places me under no obligation to buy anything. I can always return a shipment and cancel at any time. Even if I never buy another book, the two free books and gifts are mine to keep forever.

110/310 IDN F5CC

Name _____ (PLEASE PRINT)

Address _____ Apt. #

City _____ State/Prov. _____ Zip/Postal Code

Signature (if under 18, a parent or guardian must sign)

Mail to the Harlequin® Reader Service:
IN U.S.A.: P.O. Box 1867, Buffalo, NY 14240-1867
IN CANADA: P.O. Box 609, Fort Erie, Ontario L2A 5X3

Are you a current subscriber to Love Inspired Suspense books and want to receive the larger-print edition?
Call 1-800-873-8635 or visit www.ReaderService.com.

* Terms and prices subject to change without notice. Prices do not include applicable taxes. Sales tax applicable in N.Y. Canadian residents will be charged applicable taxes. Offer not valid in Quebec. This offer is limited to one order per household. Not valid for current subscribers to Love Inspired Suspense larger-print books. All orders subject to credit approval. Credit or debit balances in a customer's account(s) may be offset by any other outstanding balance owed by or to the customer. Please allow 4 to 6 weeks for delivery. Offer available while quantities last.

Your Privacy—The Harlequin® Reader Service is committed to protecting your privacy. Our Privacy Policy is available online at www.ReaderService.com or upon request from the Harlequin Reader Service.

We make a portion of our mailing list available to reputable third parties that offer products we believe may interest you. If you prefer that we not exchange your name with third parties, or if you wish to clarify or modify your communication preferences, please visit us at www.ReaderService.com/consumerschoice or write to us at Harlequin Reader Service Preference Service, P.O. Box 9062, Buffalo, NY 14269. Include your complete name and address.

LISLPDIR13R